PASSING THROUGH

R.W.K. CLARK

PRAISE FOR PASSING THROUGH

"Unputdownable!! Blood, gore, and suspense throughout. This is a book that was on my mind long after I finished it."

— *Pamela Z. Crutcher on Amazon*

"Incredibly engaging psychological thriller that you won't be able to put down."
— *Taylor on Amazon*

"Only a miracle will save them from the horror passing through."
— *Sharon Lopes*

"Very graphic and disturbing in the best way! If you like to delve into the minds of twisted, sadistic killers, you will love this book."
— *AMR on Amazon*

"A great read. The true fact is there are sickos out there just like this man."
— *Kindle Customer*

"One of the most terrifying books I've ever read scared me so much, I stayed up until I finished."
— *Cinder on Amazon*

"I cringed and kept going to the next page."
— *Gaillee on Amazon*

"The terror, the suspense, the gore... It was like watching a train wreck... you couldn't look away no matter how much you wanted to."
— *Amazon Customer*

"The pacing was fast, with an almost ominous terror building with each page."
— *Mark A Cinense on Amazon*

"Be prepared to lose sleep turning page after page long into the night."
— *Karen on Amazon*

"Humanity can sometimes bare some of the most grotesque of creatures. A pure psychological thriller."
— *John McNabb on Amazon*

"A true horror novel. It is not for the faint at heart. I have no complaints of this brilliantly written book."
— *Jerminator on Amazon*

"Sadistic, gruesome serial killer, so beware... it's very graphic, but that's what helps make the book so real."
— *Amazon Customer*

"Did I like it? No! It terrified me! Was it skillful writing? Without a doubt."
— *S.H. David on Amazon*

ACKNOWLEDGMENTS

I dedicate this novel to my beautiful readers and all the amazing people I've met and those I haven't. My family and loved ones, I will not forget all your support.

This book was made possible by reviews from readers like you.

Thank you

PROLOGUE

The young man sat, bound to the chair in front of the burning hot fireplace. He was tied tightly with a nylon rope that seemed to be cutting him in two, in more places than one. He had never felt such physical pain in his entire life.

But physical pain wasn't half of it. In front of him were three dead bodies, one his beloved girlfriend of two years. The other two girls were her friends from school. The foursome had come here for spring break fun and games. They were staying at his girlfriend's parents' cabin, a prominent, beautiful place in the snow-covered wooded mountains. It had all the makings of a perfect vacation, a little relaxing, a little partying. Between the smell of a fireplace and the cool crisp air, it was lovely.

But something went terribly wrong. Yesterday, a stranger worked his way into the home. He opened the back sliding glass door and strolled in like he owned the place.

For the next twenty-four hours, he ruthlessly tortured and tormented the group of friends.

Now, the girls lay dead, ripped open from their groins to their necks. One had her head cut nearly clean off, and each had endured hours of rape and sexual assault.

The boyfriend was forced to watch, duct tape tight over his mouth, and his eyes pinned open with large safety pins. All he could do was shake and cry as he listened to the stranger in the other room. The intruder was cooking something in the microwave and eating, and in between bites, he would sing along to a song on the radio. The kid wasn't fooling himself; when the killer was finished eating, he was sure to be next. The teenager was mentally preparing to join his girlfriend in whatever afterlife she had entered. The boy wanted to die because he would never forget a single second of what transpired, and he couldn't live with that.

Tears continued to fall down his face. He hated himself for being so powerless and weak. He thought of all the 'what ifs.' What if he had locked that damn door? What if he tried harder to overpower the man before he started his murder spree?

The radio in the kitchen went silent, and the killer rounded the corner. He stopped and stared at the three dead girls and the bloody mess left behind. A smile was glued to his face. The young man stared at the psychopath, disgusted, as he realized the man was getting aroused looking at their corpses. The boy wanted to vomit, but he would choke to death if he did. He turned away from the man to block out the deranged lunatic standing there.

"Aren't they beautiful?" the stranger asked him, amusing himself. "Oh, you would have enjoyed it all too, if you were me. You know, I was planning to off you too, young man, but now I'm full, and I'm bored. I think it's time to hit the road," so he cruelly said his goodbyes and left him sitting there in unbearable mental and physical anguish.

The still-teenaged young man did his best to scream through the tape. He was going to die there, and he knew it.

But he was wrong. A few days later, he was found by the police on the verge of death. His girlfriend's parents were worried when they hadn't heard from her. The sole spring break survivor would have to live with the terror he endured, never to forget how the three girls died in the most disturbing possible way. All the loved ones they left behind would never be the same.

ONE

"Keller!"

The inmate slowly opened his eyes but didn't move a muscle. He always maintained his composure, even when those with authority demanded control of him, as they did now. There was no reason to get all worked up and agitated. They'd just make his life more miserable. There was a particular process to all things in the penitentiary. Even something as simple as being summoned from your cell by a corrections officer for no apparent reason. He wouldn't give them any more control than they already had. As usual, he waited for the loud, hollow echo of the lock on his cell to sound, indicating they had opened it. The noise would reflect from the cold hard concrete surrounding him. It would be loud enough to wake the dead. The stench of a locker room continuously lingered in the air.

Keller awoke from the middle of a terrible dream. He could only recall bits and pieces but, in it, he was just a boy. His father had done something dreadful to his mother, maybe? He couldn't rely on his mind to play it forward or backward. Keller lost touch with reality a long time ago. He didn't know what was real and fantasy most of the time. And he had plenty of misconceptions swirling around deep in his mind. Anyway, it didn't matter. The dream was terrible, but he would've liked to know the ending or at least part of the premise. He despised when the guards, buzzers, and bells interrupted his dreams and plans.

Suddenly a metallic bang filled the air. The electronically controlled iron bolt slid from its place and slammed into the open position. Keller sat up, stretched out slowly, and swung his feet to the floor. He slid his stockinged feet into his prison-issued canvas slip-on sneakers. They were already showing signs of significant wear, even though he received a new pair just a few months ago.

Keller stood and stretched, a slight smile coming over his lips. He loved to take his time. To make them wait as long as possible, even if it was only a few extra seconds. They had too much power. It gave him some pleasure to waste as much of their time as he could for wasting his. In his mind, Keller was the one with the power. They had nothing more than illusions of grandeur, and he found it hilarious to play with them the way he did.

"Keller! Move it!" the intercom voice echoed throughout the corridor.

He stepped up to the door of his cell and waited a few seconds just for spite. Then he stepped out into the cold tile and cinder block corridor. Following protocol, he stopped, put his hands behind his back, and stared straight ahead. It was the kind of policy that seemed like overkill.

The door reversed, slamming loudly against the end of its track. Several other inmates, whose cells were running along the same side of the hall, began to grumble for being disturbed, either from naps, reading, or perverted behavior. He paid them no mind. He shut out their voices because they were simply irrelevant.

Keller resumed his straight-posture position, clasping his hands behind him. It was just after suppertime, around six-thirty in the evening. He stared out the windows which lined the bare cinder block wall across from the row of cells. The sky was beginning to darken early now, and soon, there would be no light left in the day. November, December, and January had always been his favorite months because of the early, long-lasting darkness at night. It gave men like him plenty of time to have fun under the cover of the night. Nighttime was the best time to play if you were easily bored.

"Turn right and approach the door!" The intercom-streamed voice echoed once again, this time a bit softer.

Like a loyal soldier, Keller did as he was told and proceeded to walk down the long corridor, past the other cells. He ignored the vile comments slung in his direction from other offenders. Keller wasn't there to make friends. Bunch of juvenile sissies, he thought to himself.

At the far end of the corridor was a massive, heavy door, constructed entirely of thick steel, and like everything else in prison, it was painted their standard-policy gray. There was a small window in the door about a foot-and-a-half from the top that measured eight inches by eight inches. It held a pane of glass reinforced with wire on the inside. Like all the others at the Virginia Maximum Correctional Institution, this door was controlled electronically by a prison guard who sat in a glass bubble on the other side. As he waited for them to buzz him through, Keller muttered under his breath about how rough it must be to sit on your fat ass eating donuts all day long giving orders.

The door buzzed obnoxiously, prompting him to grab it by the handle and give it a violent tug. The latch popped audibly, stopping the profane buzzing. Keller pulled it all the way open and stepped through, letting it slam shut and hearing it automatically lock behind him.

One of the best-known corrections officers was standing there in all his glory, his brown and tan uniform tightly hugging his pot belly. He stood about six-foot-four and was completely bald. He had a nicely groomed handlebar mustache that seemed to trickle down from his upper lip to his chin on both sides. The man smirked in Keller's direction.

"Follow me. We have a change in your work assignment, and there are quite a few things to go over before you can begin tonight."

Keller was silent. He simply followed the robust man like he was told. His mind raced with slurs, and bloody thoughts of what Keller would do to this particular man if ever alone with him and the circumstances were right. These people had no idea what he was capable of. They had seen pictures and heard testimonies given by whimpering lowlifes who were blackened by their sins, just never caught. To the prison staff, most crimes were surreal. They couldn't fully grasp the insidiousness because they never witnessed it for themselves. Their jobs began after the blood, guts, and hearings. They just showed up for work every day, dealt with the scumbags, armed with their guns and sticks and chains. Then they went home to their wives and kids—what a dull existence.

They continued walking down several cold hallways, past several doors, and finally stopped outside the Inmate Work Detail office, which was in the admin section of the main building. The administrators were gone this time of day; they shot out the door at five o'clock like a cannon. That left the prison guards to come and go in the office area. Whatever the reason for summoning him was a last-minute matter.

The officer unlocked the department door and held it, signifying that Keller should enter with a nod. He did, then stood still and silent, waiting to be told what to do next. The guard walked around the desk in the middle of the small office, sat down, then gruffly nodded toward a chair; Keller sat.

"Our night laundry guy had some trouble on the job, so he lost it," the C.O. began. He was sitting back in the chair with his arms crossed over his chest. "Now, we all know who you are and what you're accused of and capable of, but your boss, the sergeant, seems to think that you can be trusted to take the position. First, the lieutenant wants me to give you a thorough interview... get a good read on you before we move you up. This laundry shift requires trust, Keller. Now, I admit, you've kept your nose good and clean for the last five years, but you're a freaking animal, and we both know it. So, tell me. Why should we let you be alone for eight hours a night down in laundry? Why should we trust you with Reception & Delivery?"

Keller didn't smile, but he sure wanted to. He couldn't believe his ears. Were they going to offer him the night shift? The guard had just asked a good question. Why would they let him have the position? Were they all out of their minds? He had been eager to nab that shift for years, but not because he was trying to move up the inmate corporate ladder. He thought about his answer. His eyes skimmed from the officer to the items on the desk and back again. He memorized everything on the desk because there were only two: a file folder and one lonely sheet of paper. No pen holders, no desk lamp, not even a blotter. Oh, yeah. That's right. He was in prison. He chuckled silently to himself and mentally shook his head.

"You know, mister, I've thought about how nice that night shift would be lots of times." Inmate Keller clicked his tongue against his cheek. "I don't think there's a man here who hasn't. So, this is my reward for being a 'good boy'? Well, I have to say, I'm much obliged, sir. The fact is, if I'm spending the rest of my life here, I may as well make it as pleasant for myself as possible, even if that includes little promotions here and there. I mean, if the tables were turned, wouldn't you do the same?"

The officer didn't smile or nod. He was busy studying the convict across from him, wondering if his calm, controlled demeanor could be trusted in any way. He had been a guard with the state prison system for nearly twenty years, and he hadn't met a prisoner yet who uttered a single word you could believe. Even the octogenarian lifers they housed were as slippery as eels if you turned your back on them. Judging from the horrific facts pertaining to Elliot Keller's crimes, he was no different from any of them. Perhaps much worse.

"Well, the tables aren't turned. Quite frankly, you deserve death, but instead, well, here we are."

VIRGINIA MAX WAS A MAXIMUM-SECURITY prison and one of the most secure in the nation. A sizeable old estate building stood where the prison did now. But it had been razed and replaced with consistent upgrades as technology improved over the years. This prison could contain the vermin that lived behind its razor wires and armed guard towers.

Virginia supported the death penalty, but Keller avoided that particular consequence by the skin of his teeth. Though not overly bright, he had a way of buttering up those in charge. Keller knew precisely how to quietly, very quietly, schmooze the right people. Make them second-guess just how dangerous a man he was with his controlled demeanor. The guard didn't want to know what made the man tick. That would mean diving down to his level of insanity, and he wasn't interested. He would take a hard pass on being a counselor or group leader. He preferred trying to keep these rabid dirtballs in line. He hoped he'd get a chance, or two, to bust a cap in them before he retired.

His eyes continued to scan Keller, up and down, considering every angle of trouble the man could get into on laundry duty. Nothing would surprise him with this guy.

———

KELLER WAS A TRIPLE MURDERER. HE KILLED three innocent young women who were spring break vacationing at a cabin belonging to one of the girls' parents. It had been six years since the brutal slayings. It was supposed to be a fun, footloose time for the four young adults, but it turned into a nightmare when Keller happened to come upon the cabin after breaking down near one of the Appalachian Trailheads. He had just hiked himself out of the national scenic trail when he stumbled upon the cabin. Keller slipped through the unlocked, sliding glass door and pounced like a hungry wildcat. Armed and bored, by his admission, the man took the kids hostage in the cabin, forcing them into submission with fear for their lives. Keller bound the young man, tied him to a chair, and forced him to watch as he shot each of the young ladies in the foot, disabling them. He proceeded to beat each of the girls with the butt of his gun, then rape them repeatedly while the young man was forced to watch in horror. Keller placed safety pins through the boy's eyelids, then taped them up with duct tape. He ran the tape in two long strips that went over the top of his head and down his back. The young man miraculously survived the ordeal, testifying that Keller let him live because he had grown bored of their games, and after such a good time, he was tired. Keller left him there, tied to the chair in front of the bodies. The owners couldn't reach them after calling multiple times over an entire day. They were all discovered by the State Patrol. Captain Russell Johnson was first on the scene.

THINKING ABOUT WHAT KELLER HAD DONE TO those kids made him want to put the hurt on him something awful. He couldn't fathom why the sergeant thought this guy was right for the job. To have control over the laundry room, alone, every night. He deserved to sit in his cell and rot.

Sure, there was no way of escaping, with an officer coming and going to observe deliveries and the basic operations. But to work in the laundry was also a privilege. Inmates came in contact with outsiders, such as deliverymen, food truck drivers, US Mail carriers, and countless others. The prison was a tiny working town, so to speak. High fences and razor wire also surrounded it, all electrified. At every junction in the wall around the property stood a manned guard in each tower, alert and armed. Lights were everywhere, and at the first hint of a breach, deafening alarms would blare.

The guard's problem with Keller getting the job was

simple. The man was a monster, and he didn't deserve it. He should've received the death penalty for such acts, but thanks to a smooth-talking expert psychiatrist as a witness, he dodged that bullet. The shrink loaded him up with medication and gave a persuasive expert opinion on the stand about his mental illness. So, he was put here by the great state of Virginia. He was a psychotic degenerate who should be far from other human beings. But, as the jury found, he was also too insane to put down. Keller is a rabid dog, a poisonous snake, neither of which can ever be trusted.

But Warden Jaffrey called the ultimate shots, and this 'promotion' was her call all the way. She even seemed enthusiastic about it. Wanda Jaffrey was reasonably new to the position, having just taken over as warden two short years ago. She also happened to be the first female warden Virginia Max had ever known, and she had some pretty flighty ideas when it came to convicts and rehabilitation. Wanda wanted to give a little trust, to get a little responsibility, even inside the walls of a prison that housed the most violent criminals in the state, some in the world. Even though the inmates here would likely never see the light of day, she believed they could live meaningful and happy lives, free of their violence and burdens, through rehabilitation. Maybe so, but how would anybody ever really know? What's sincere with these people, and what's a mask? These inmates were sick and hardened, many with a long list of previous offenses.

They would do it again in a heartbeat and rip her to shreds if given a chance.

But in the end, the corrections officer was just a guard, and he was there to carry the crap downhill instead of allowing it to roll. It didn't help that they were in a crunch to fill the position. The previous night laundry worker, who did a great job over the last eight years, tried to commit suicide. His wife of twenty-five years decided she couldn't live loyally to a convict, a quarter-century in or not. She 'Dear John-ed' him, leaving the warden no choice.

After several long, quiet minutes of thought, the officer offered more of a smirk than a half-smile and clasped his hands in front of him on the desk. He was never really one to pull punches, and he had no favorites nor pets when it came to these losers. Not even the small-timers could get in his good graces. Oh, he could be pleasant enough, but his pleasantries went no deeper than the sound of his voice. He despised them. He hated them all, and if it were up to him, not one of them would exist on the planet.

"Warden Jaffrey seems to think you're the shoo-in, Keller. You've got her snowed, though I don't get how you managed to do it. I don't believe you have enough time under your belt for such a trusted position, but I don't run the show. You're going to die here, Keller. But not after wasting years of taxpayer dollars. You're excrement to me and nothing more."

The corrections officer paused and held the murderer's eyes for effect. The prisoner held his steadily and calmly in return, no expression on his face. "But on record, and even I must admit, you haven't had a behavior problem of any kind, not from the beginning. Some may find that reassuring. Not me; I think it makes you dangerous. Silent but deadly. You cooperated when you were arrested and did everything right during your trial. You've given us no trouble, not in jail, not as much of a whimper since you transferred here. No fights. No physical or verbal attacks. Not even a complaint about the food. For someone who did what you did, well, I just can't figure you out, except to guess that you've got something up your prison-issued sleeve. So, because of your self-control and steady cooperation with our prison program. And because I don't have a thing to say about it, the job is yours. We need you to start tonight at eleven. Be sure to watch the clock because none of us are going to do you any favors by waking you up. We're all hoping you oversleep and get fired before you ever set foot down there tonight."

Keller offered a smile, though it was tight around the edges. He sat forward, his elbows resting on his thighs.

"Well, sir, you tell the warden I said thank you. I know she's a busy woman. So, I won't bother her." An expectant look crossed his face, but he remained silent until the guard stood.

But the officer didn't stand. He held Keller's gaze.

Giving him the job was a mistake; he just knew it. Aside from the obvious, he didn't know why the guy bothered him more than any other inmate. No, it was the man himself. To put it simply, the C.O. didn't trust him as far as he could throw him.

"Tell me something, Keller," the officer finally said in a strong but controlled voice. "Why'd you do it?"

Now a sincere smile came over the murderer's face, and the prison guard watched his eyes soften a bit. "Now, you know as well as anyone else on the face of the earth. Why do we cause ourselves any trouble, big or small? Why do we drive drunk, hit our wives, shoplift, or even torture little, insignificant animals for entertainment? I'll tell you exactly why, Boss.

Because sometimes, messing up is simply a lot more fun and entertaining than anything else you have going on at the time. Sometimes, you do it because you can."

TWO

T he cell door gave its signature slam behind Keller as he crossed the tiny area he called home. Reaching his bunk, he sat down and stared out through the bars and zoned in on a cinder block. Since coming to Virginia Max, he looked for the same one each day, as if it were a friend. He was most fond of that one, but he had all the blocks memorized. Every crack or chipped paint spot... each difference was etched into his mind like a fond memory, not that he had any of those. Keller used the block and its details to focus and calm himself when he felt the urge to blow, more often than anyone in prison knew. He would stare at the block every day and shut everything out that ate away at him. He did it for however long it took to calm his pounding heart and screaming rage. The block was his rock. No matter where he was at any moment within the facility, he could turn his mind over to it and temporarily reduce his desires—playing with the blood and guts of another inmate or guard. It was a lifesaver in more ways than one. To put it simply, the block kept him from continuing his rampages, kept him out of the hole, and had ultimately gotten him the night laundry position he wanted for so long.

He couldn't believe the time had finally come, but it had. Keller waited patiently, biding his time and subtly kissing up to prison staff by simply minding his p's and q's in hopes of landing the much-desired night laundry position. Now it was his! He had the sergeant, lieutenant, and most of all, the warden completely fooled. All of his mental hard work, focusing, and refusing the joy and fun he wanted were paying off, resulting in the promotion. Tonight, at ten-forty-five, a guard would escort him to laundry. Soon, that position would spell out freedom. His plans would work. It would just take the right timing and fine-tuning of the details. He had nothing but time and had learned the attribute of patience. After all, he had been in prison for nearly five years on top of time spent waiting for meetings, hearings, and trials. Yes, if doing time did anything for a man, it taught him patience, but only if he let it.

A mixed bag of other life experiences did the same for him over the years. Like the times his biological father locked him in the dank storage area on the dirt floor in the basement when he was two or three years old. He preferred that method when Keller dribbled on the toilet seat or walked around with one of his shoes untied. The man was a brute. His punishments had nothing to do with actual discipline or the desire to have a well-behaved son. No, the elder Keller got off on all the screaming, crying, and begging that his tactics incited. Sometimes, his father would even sit in a metal folding chair outside of the room in the basement, laughing and eating platefuls of aromatic food prepared by his bloodied and beaten mother. His father would ask him, over and over as he laughed, if he thought the fried chicken smelled good, and wouldn't he just love some?

Keller vowed he'd kill the scumbag someday, and he would do the same to his mother, just for letting it happen.

He broke his dead stare and slipped off his shoes, then lay down on his bed. He listened to the sounds of the other inmates who lived on M Corridor, which was his own. Someone was shuffling a deck of cards, and he could hear a low conversation of men sharing war stories of crime. Now and then, a snicker or full laugh could be heard out of them. Convicts loved to boast of their conquests, trying to one-up each other. But he knew better than to share. Plus, his adventures in life were his own, and he treasured each act in his mental diary. It's all he had for now, and he would share them with no one.

The cards were being shuffled again. Often, the inmates in two neighboring cells would get together where their cells met and converse or play dice or cards through the bars, using the corridor floor as their table. The inmates on M Corridor were not supposed to have this kind of joint playtime. They were considered the worst and segregated unless on job detail or taking rehabilitative classes and counseling. Suddenly, Keller laughed aloud, and the jackasses with the cards went silent for a second hearing him. Keller snicked at their curiosity and waited for the shuffling to begin once again.

Everyone at Virginia Max was crazy, in their own way and on their level. No one did the things these men did without being 'off.' Period. Just because they were mentally ill didn't necessarily mean they weren't aware of the difference between right and wrong. Even Elliot Keller knew that anyone who raped and murdered was deranged, even if they did it simply to get off on it. Yeah, he was nuts, and he was dangerous, and he loved every single minute of it. The look in the eyes of his victims was like a fine hollandaise poured over fresh asparagus. Their screams were like a perfectly grilled medium-rare Porterhouse. Their deaths were his idea of winning the lottery, and the precious memories got his rocks off with such potency that he trembled when he thought about them. He loved to reminisce about the good old days.

Yes, he was feared, and he was keenly aware of it, though he had done nothing to instigate the emotion in other inmates. His reputation preceded him, and it was as simple as that. He kept to himself, never intentionally intimidating or threatening anyone on the inside. The only communication he had with others was out of need or force. For instance, working with counselors requires communication, both in a group or one-on-one sessions. To him, these interactions were all business, not therapy at all. He carefully chose his words and kept them on topic. Keller never offered information about himself to other prisoners; he wasn't here to make friends. The only time he spoke about his accused crime, or any other he had committed, was in these sessions. When Keller talked, his words were brief, extremely calculated, and superficial. It was essential to appear remorseful and repentant to gain their trust, so he gave them just enough to satisfy them. There was much more going on in his mind, however. As he divulged details, he simultaneously imagined what he'd do to every one of them. He was never connected emotionally to anything that came out of his mouth.

He was never attached to anyone, and Keller liked it that way. They didn't need to know any more about him than they already did. After all, they carried around little textbooks, which they studied to place him in the appropriate category to analyze his criminal mind. They profiled him as any good criminal psychologist should, but none had it right. But they were close enough. He knew if he revealed too much, his plans would be spoiled. So, he threw them off their trails and made them guess, changing the course of his rehabilitation more than once. He kept his darkest thoughts all to himself.

His mind drifted to the laundry job again. When he first arrived at Virginia Max, his assigned work detail was lousy. He worked in the prison kitchen, where all newcomers started. Dishwashing came first, then up to floors and deep cleaning. If you didn't ruffle feathers, moving up was easy, and it hadn't taken him long before he was put in charge of the dry storage room, a cushy job.

There were those in the world, many men and women just like Keller. But none of them had the nerve to bring their dreams and fantasies to life the way he did. Keller was the real deal. He was faithful to himself and his mind. If they didn't get it while they sat up on their high horses and pointed down at him, judging and shaking their heads, they never would.

He would love nothing more than to show them what went through a crazed criminal mind like his, what it could do.

His thoughts shifted back to the institution itself, the place he called home for the last several years. Keller really couldn't complain about Virginia Max, regardless of all the technicalities and phonies. Of all the prisons in the state, this was the most comfortable. He considered the level of security and offenders inside its walls. The majority of inmates were violent, and most of them were doing twenty-five to life or even multiple life sentences. Of course, that was assuming they weren't on death row.

Not all of them escaped the death penalty as he did. The place consisted of corridor units, housing the most violent or the criminally insane. Those who couldn't be trusted lived along these corridors because they were classified as 'unable to cohabitate with others peacefully.' Other prisoners were housed in separate block units depending on their crimes. They were mid-level criminals who were usually serving fifteen to twenty-five. They were men who had a light at the end of their tunnel. Men who just might see freedom before they died. Whether or not they could control themselves to remain free was a whole other story.

Virginia Max also had inmates who were housed in the psychiatric unit. Their crimes were attributed to their mental state, so they were pumped full of drugs and put in restraints while they did their time. On occasion, they could go out into an enclosed yard with grass and benches. But they were heavily watched so they didn't do anything to hurt themselves or others. Some of these men would get out, but most would die in the stinking, filthy unit they lived in.

A handful of men were in the 'hole.' They went in and out, in and out, doing their hole time for some infraction or other, getting back into the population, then doing something else. They were defiant and didn't have the brains to know when to shut their mouths. They were the attention seekers who would act up just to make their friends laugh. Keller didn't have that problem. He had been doing time in one way or another since he was born.

But now, after five years, he could see the light at the end of his own tunnel, one he would find on his own. He wasn't sure of the specific details and hadn't yet formed a solid plan, but his new laundry position was his ticket out of Virginia Max. It might take a week or maybe a month; it could take a year or more. It didn't matter how long it took, Keller was going to walk out of this place, and he was going to make the absolute most of it when he did. They would catch him again eventually, but that would be okay. It was his duty to escape. What kind of criminal didn't think about and attempt to escape from a life sentence?

Keller closed his eyes and steadied his mind. He wasn't going to just *try* to break out from prison, he would get the job done. Once they caught him and faced the new charges, Keller would return with a smile on his face. He would come back with a brand-new memory reel full of warm blood and terrifying screams etched into his heart forever.

THREE

Another snowstorm was about to hit the town of Thompson Trails, and it was promising to be a doozy. The town was on emergency alert, and though the snow was barely just beginning to fall, the entire population had already bought provisions, preparing for the worst. Milk, eggs, and bread were swept from the shelves, as well as wine and beer. All the staples necessary for being snowed in, especially at this time of year.

It was the start of the holiday season, so many residents were also leaving. Some were coming to see family for Thanksgiving. With the storm brewing, folks altered plans to reach their destinations ahead of time. A single bus was scheduled to arrive for one final drop-off and pick-up. The rest would be canceled until the storm was over and the roads were cleared.

Sheriff Robert Brown, known as Bob to the locals, loved his town. When inclement weather hit, he always made it a habit to check in on the residents, especially those most vulnerable. He was paying his visits while the bus arrived for its final Thompson Trails stop.

Sheriff Brown pulled down a gravel lane toward the Martin cabin. The snow was beginning to cover the drive with a fine dusting. He climbed out of his truck and knocked on the door. The Martins lived in the big, beautiful cabin year-round, and they refused to leave, even in adverse conditions. He just wanted to make sure they had everything they needed.

"Howdy, Bob," Jake Martin welcomed as he opened the door and let the Sheriff in.

"Mornin'," Sheriff Brown greeted the family and nodded at Janet Martin, who was crocheting next to the fire. Their fifteen-year-old daughter was engrossed with something on her smartphone. "Just stopping to check-in. You know, it's going to be a bad one. I assume you've been following the predictions?"

"Worst one yet," Jake replied. "We're just gonna stay in and bond, if you know what I mean."

Bob nodded. "Best bet for us all, I think. Smells good in here. What did you all have for breakfast?"

"Biscuits... ugh," their daughter replied, with a crinkle of her nose.

The adults laughed.

"Can I get you a coffee, Bob?" Janet asked.

"No, thank you, ma'am," he replied. "Much obliged, but I still have several families to check in on, and the missus is expecting me on time for dinner."

"Be sure to give Rose our love," Janet replied.

Jake made his way to the door to show the sheriff out. "Sure, appreciate your concern. We're all going to have to get together for some canasta when this passes."

"Sounds good to me," Bob said with a tip of his hat. "Well, I'm out of here. Lock 'er up and keep safe, y'all."

He returned to his truck, turned around, and headed back up the drive. The snow was coming down good now. Huge flakes fell on the windshield so big that Bob could make out some of their patterns. And the wind was picking up, moving the snow sideways at times. During the short time he had been there, the snow had accumulated at least an inch.

"Yep, it's a bad one, all right," he muttered as he pulled out of the drive and onto the highway.

DONNA WELK TURNED THE KEY IN THE KEYHOLE of the office door and rushed inside, slamming the door quickly behind her. She stopped and let out the long, ragged breath she'd been holding. Then she brushed the snow off the shoulders of her parka and hung it on the hook behind the main desk. Sitting down, she shivered once more, still feeling the chill from outside. If the weather was like this in Virginia the first week of November, she dreaded what the rest of winter would be like.

She quickly glanced at the clock: nine-fifteen in the morning. Donna highly doubted that they would have any guests today because of the weather. Usually, this time of year, the flow of guests was slow but steady. But as of that moment, Donna and her husband didn't have a single cabin rented out, and she couldn't foresee any interest, certainly not today. If the weatherman were right, they would likely be empty for the remainder of the week. It would hurt the pocketbook, but it was better than people risking their lives to rent a cabin near the Appalachian Trail. Guests would wait; life did not.

She and Rick had purchased the old cluster of cabins two years ago, both with big dreams of taking the trailhead at Thompson Trails by storm. The business, and the cottages, still needed a lot of work. Guest accommodations were in need of renovation, everything from new beds to new showers. Also, the business itself was racking up some debt that would take months, if not two years, to pay off. But they were making progress; last year, they remodeled the outside of all the units and freshly landscaped the grounds. They also added a small playground for kids and set up a station for guests to rent canoes, paddleboats, and beach supplies for the lake behind the cabins. After promoting specials for new and returning guests, they began to climb out of the hole. In the beginning, getting back in the black was an overwhelming prospect. Now it looked like things would be cleared up in the next eighteen months.

"But not if we have many days like this," Donna muttered as she pulled out the checkbook to pay the bills.

The small town of Thompson Trails knew the storm was on its way, but they all hoped it would either dissipate or pass before it reached them. It hadn't, and last night the first flakes began to fall. When Donna and Rick woke in the morning, the town was covered in a blanket of glistening white snow. Rick quickly dressed and retrieved the snowblower to clear the lot for potential guests. It was possible to gain a few who may be stranded, so they wanted to be prepared for anything.

Donna got down to business in the office. No sooner did she turn the space heater on, Rick rushed through the door. The wind fought him hard as he tried to close it. He turned around and leaned against the door, his face red and breathing labored.

"I needed a break, or I was going to blow away!" He unzipped his coat and started to remove it. "Why don't you have the radio on? They said the main road through town would be closing in a few hours; the snow is going to last for days! They're going to close the interstate both ways until the snow begins to die down so they can clear the roads!"

Donna groaned, sat back in her desk chair, and turned on the radio. "Don't bother with all that snowplowing right now. It's too dangerous. We're right in the middle of the storm! Well, so much for any guests for a day or two. I guess now's the time for me to catch up on getting those hard files on the computer, eh?"

"Good idea. You know, you'll probably scan all those old records in, and then ten years from now, we'll realize that we never even looked at them once." Rick hung up his coat and rubbed his hands together. "At least the lot is clear for now, you know, just in case we get lucky or something in the very near future."

Donna chuckled and shook her head. "Ever the optimist, my husband."

"Someone has to be. Say, maybe if it stays like this, we can participate together in a little, you know, hanky-panky."

Donna turned and grabbed one of three boxes of files stacked out of sight behind her desk. There were more than twenty when they bought the place, and she only had three left. The previous owners hadn't used computers or technology for recordkeeping, and now Donna was cleaning up the mess.

With a shake of her head, she replied, "This is all the hanky-panky I'm getting into today."

"Well, Dear, I'm going to warm up then hit that lot again." He paused, seeing Donna's look of disapproval. "Now, don't argue. I'll be fine, and it's better to stay on top of it." He paused and glanced at the guest courtesy table, which sat behind him in the lobby. The table offered packaged donuts, cookies, fruit, and coffee. "You didn't make any java? Woman! Do you want any?"

"If you're making it."

Rick stuck his tongue out and grabbed the pot. Donna watched her husband fondly as he filled it with water, then scooped coffee into the basket. Regardless of the work and the cost, she believed they made an excellent decision when they bought the Virginia Trailhead Cabins. If nothing else, the purchase and move took their minds off the recent loss of pregnancy and the subsequent knowledge that there would be no more chances of parenting for them. Their final attempt was In Vitro, after several years of trying with multiple doctors and fertility medications. Donna and Rick took the news poorly but were just starting to come to terms with it. They decided to forget about having children and buy the cabins. She didn't believe it was a mistake. The couple made the small lake getaway near the Appalachian Trail their child instead. It was their baby, and they cared for it as such. Donna and Rick found happiness after a terrible loss. Sometimes, when Rick brought up lovemaking, as he just did, her stomach turned. It wasn't that she didn't like fooling around, but for some reason, she couldn't separate it from childbearing, and they both knew that wasn't going to happen for them. It was heartbreaking, not being able to have kids. It was something she knew she had to work through.

The small cabin resort had changed their lives for the

better. Rick and Donna relocated, started life anew, and made new friends. It didn't take them long to fit right in, and now they were considered 'locals' by the others, which tickled them. The handful of native Thompson Trails residents didn't take kindly to new settlers. It was a well-known fact. But for some reason, the couple fit right in, like a couple of toes in a nicely broken-in shoe.

They both went about their tasks, with Rick making coffee and Donna focusing on the paperwork and the computer. The sudden sound of tires crunching over the rapidly accumulating snow grabbed her attention, and she turned to the window. Sheriff Robert Brown was pulling into the lot in his big pickup plow. Donna wasn't surprised. The short, stocky man liked to touch base with his people when the weather acted up, just in case they needed anything and to evaluate their safety.

She turned her head to see her husband coming out of the men's room, fastening his belt. "Bob's outside. Better ask him in for some coffee."

Grabbing his coat, he replied, "Sure thing." Rick opened the office door and stepped outside, waving his arm at the sheriff. Donna heard him shout, "Hey, Bob! A beautiful day we're having!"

Donna turned her attention back to her work with a smile and a shake of her head. Even amidst a storm, she felt at peace. Of all the hardships and decisions Donna faced with Rick during their marriage, moving to Thompson Trails was definitely the best one they made.

"So, I was told a resort company out of Richmond was planning to level the old grocery building to put a strip mall in. They say it will bring more business to the small town and give it a bigger dot on the maps. You know what, Rose? Believe it or not, I think Darren got the last thing I put on the list for him to pick up from Donneley's Pass," Avery Rush said, with a smile on her face.

This made Rose Brown Happy. "Usually, he forgot at least something, but he's been so good lately about taking care of me. Sometimes I feel guilty about it."

Rose patted her on the shoulder. "Just try to understand he loves you."

Avery understood the stress. It had made her physically ill to have to tell her husband she was pregnant. Darren Rush was carrying around a lot of responsibilities already. Being the deputy was a hard job, and now, they were pregnant and needed a bigger house to boot.

She couldn't do anything to stop the onslaught of her husband's responsibilities, and now there was a child on the way. To make it worse, she had been consistently ill during the pregnancy, but in the last couple of weeks, Avery was beginning to feel better.

She sat with Rose, drinking coffee while going through the cards for the baby shower that Darren had brought her from Donneley's Pass. As she said, it appeared he had gotten every last item on the list.

"Avery, don't you forget about that appointment you have at noon with Dr. Frazer," Rose said, in a motherly fashion. "I know you're feeling better. I can tell, but I think you must follow through in this situation, dear. Who knows? Maybe he'll tell you if it's a boy or a girl?"

Avery glanced at her watch. "Yes, I should go home and jump into the shower, I suppose. Listen, don't you worry a thing about all these cards. As soon as I get back, I'll give you a call. I need to do a bit more unpacking as well. Tomorrow we can get back to work, and soon, the cards will be out of your hair." She turned to the lady and brought her in for a hug. Rose embraced her back hard.

"You're a great help," she said. "You know as well as I do that I wouldn't have made it through all of this without you and Bob."

"I know dear, now scoot."

Avery gave the woman a peck on the cheek and disappeared home.

An hour later, Avery was leaving the house with her husband, who had returned to drive her to her appointment in Donneley's Pass.

Darren sat in the waiting room at Dr. Frazer's office, waiting patiently for his wife with a magazine in his lap. He wasn't reading it, just blindly flipping the pages every few minutes. His mind was on Avery. Over the last few weeks, she had been a hot mess with all the morning sickness. In addition to her physical discomfort, it affected her state of mind. She never thought it would end, but she seemed a bit better as of late. She is much more cheerful, like she might be getting back to her original self.

The door to the examination rooms opened, and Avery stepped out. She looked a little pale, but a smile covered her face when she saw Darren. He smiled back and stood up.

"All done?" he asked.

"Just about," she replied softly. "Dr. Frazer wants me to make a follow-up appointment. If you want to go start the truck, I'll be out in just a bit."

Darren nodded and left, Avery watching him as he went. She turned to the pretty young receptionist. "The doctor wants me to schedule another appointment."

The girl looked up at her cheerfully. "I know, dear. He filled me in. I'm glad you're feeling better. When's a good time for you?"

The two women narrowed down a time, working around all the chores Darren and Avery had on their plate due to their pending move. Avery kept a smile on her face the entire time, but she felt like she was falling apart inside. When they were finished, she tucked the little appointment card in her purse, plastered another smile on, and went out to join her waiting husband.

As they drove back to Thompson Trails, Darren was eager to hear about her appointment. "Wow, this snow is coming down fast. So, what did Dr. Frazer say?"

"Well," Avery replied lightly, "he thinks I'm doing better, both mentally and physically."

"Great!" Darren rubbed her thigh. "So, what's the follow-up for?"

Avery shrugged and picked at some invisible lint on her coat. "Just to make sure my body is handling the change all right, I guess."

"What a relief!" Darren fondled her leg again. "I sure love you. I have to tell you, you are the best woman I know, and I'm so lucky to have you."

"I feel the same way about you. Now slow down. We have a baby on board."

They tooled the rest of the way back to their new home with the radio on, humming and holding hands with each passing mile. Darren seemed happy enough; Avery glanced at him the rest of the way home out of the corner of her eye, smiling.

THE RUSHES GOT HOME FROM DONNELEY'S PASS late that afternoon. Avery had spent the remainder of the day unpacking and sorting. While she worked, Darren was transporting boxes and other small items to their new home. With each return trip, he would pile more stuff into the truck. Rose had given them several items of furniture she was storing, and it gave the Rush's an excellent start. It should all be perfect for them both. Tonight, all the moving would be done, and after Darren returned with the last load, the two would have pizza together, which was Darren's idea.

Around seven-thirty that evening, Darren returned from the final run. He could see a fire burning in the fireplace, and the other light on in the house was coming from the main bedroom.

"I'm back, babe. The snow is getting deep," he hollered when he walked through the door. "I have a loaded pizza. Did you pick a movie?"

He put the food items on the dining room table and removed his coat. "Babe? Where are you? I'm back!"

Darren looked in the kitchen, peeked out through the door leading to the garage, checked the bathroom, and finally made his way down the hall to their room. Avery was sitting up on the bed with pillows propped behind her back when he opened the door. She wore a white silk gown, and her hair was brushed and styled to perfection. There were a dozen or so lit candles around the room.

"Hello, love," Avery said softly, smiling at him.

"I take it you have some pretty big plans for tonight." Darren grinned.

She nodded, then gestured with her right hand to the bed. "I have something for you."

Darren walked to the foot of the bed and sat on the edge. "What's this?"

"You'll have to come to find out." The tone of her voice excited him; his heart began to pound.

"I love you."

She didn't answer. She just stared at Darren's face smiling and said, "Get over here."

THE WELKS MADE THEIR WAY OUT THE BACK door of their cabin to an enclosed hot tub. They hurried, hand in hand, to the very inviting spa. "I can't wait to get in," Donna said with excitement.

"I can't wait to see you naked." Rick gushed with a smile. Sometimes he missed what Donna said as he was too busy with her enchanting eyes. They were the first thing he ever noticed about her. Some people have wonderful eyes. Of course, it wasn't just her eyes that distracted him. Not right now, anyway. She had already kicked her shoes off and was unbuttoning her jeans. Soon, she was standing there in a bra and panties. He'd forgotten about her eyes for the moment, magnificent as they may be. The rest of the evening was perfect. They took off the rest of their clothes and sat in the hot, whirling bath. After an uncomfortable minute, the water felt fantastic on their bodies.

At that point, Donna didn't know if she ever wanted to get out of the hot bath. They kissed and held each other, then splashed around like a couple of kids on vacation. They kissed some more. Donna whispered to Rick that she loved him and wanted his hands to caress her all over... and not to stop. Rick loved to spoil his wife. Rubbing and kissing her was just as pleasurable for him. Afterward, they lay on a blanket in front of the fireplace. Rick looked down at her, nestled in the curve of his body by the fire. She seemed so soft and vulnerable.

Eventually, the two dressed and fixed some dinner. The Welks were feeling relaxed and happy. A long day's work was just a memory. The blizzard was an only mild concern.

FOUR

Two weeks later

Elliot Keller sat rigidly on his bunk, waiting to be called out of the cell for his overnight laundry work detail. His face was devoid of expression, his hands resting calmly in his lap. His mind, however, was not still. It focused solely on the night ahead of him, for it would consist of much more than washing, drying, folding, and signing for deliveries.

"Keller!"

Without hesitation, he moved forward and stopped dead before the door as it slid open on its track, culminating in a metallic bang as it reached the end. Keller stepped forward and took the same position, hands clasped behind his back in the corridor. The door reversed, closed, and slammed into place behind him once again. Soon, he was making his way up the passageway toward the metal door at the end, ignoring the loud, obnoxious snores coming from the other men on M Corridor. He had far more critical things complicating his mind.

The door popped, and Keller jerked it open so he could pass through. As it slammed shut behind him, a night-shift correctional officer named Kolchak rounded the corner, pulling his black latex gloves taut against his fingers. Keller studied him as he approached his pathetic shuffle, the downcast eyes. He hates his job and all the terrible people in prison. Keller smiled on the inside but maintained his stoic façade on the outside.

"Ready, Keller?"

Keller took the front, walking so that the escort could keep his eyes on the inmate from behind. With his hands clasped behind his back per prison policy, Keller strolled at a steady, even pace in silence. The escorting officer finally broke the silence.

"From what I hear, you've taken to nightshift laundry like a fish to water," Kolchak remarked in a friendly, conversational tone. "I gotta say, I'm glad to hear it. I thought you'd be the perfect man for the job, the way you keep to yourself and all, you know?"

"Thank you for that, Officer Kolchak."

The middle-aged man cleared his throat lightly. "No problem. Once you're in a place like this, that's punishment enough, I say. You might as well go on and try to live out your life the best you can. I know a lot of people think that, well, you ought to be dead and all, but I figure the Man upstairs would have made that happen if that's what he wanted. I know you ain't a praying man, but you know what I mean, right Keller?"

"Yes, sir. I surely do." He couldn't help but laugh to himself—what a joke. The only gods on this planet were the men who stood up and made things happen the way they wanted to. Most of them were politicians, but the rest of them were like him. Yes, he was a god, all right.

Keller continued to walk, with Kolchak humming a little tune as they moved. As far as prison guards went, Keller thought this one was a good one, just here to do his job. No personal agendas. No politics. No ulterior motives. At that moment, the inmate found himself relieved that this officer would not be the one looking in on him or monitoring late-night delivery drop-offs. This one didn't deserve what was to come, but others did.

"So, sir, who's going to be my supervisor tonight, do you know?" Keller's voice was polite and respectful, just the way it ought to be. It was the perfect way to maintain a smooth rapport with officers like Kolchak. As long as you did what you were supposed to, they continued to treat you like a human being, even if you weren't very human at all.

"Hmm, lemme see." The C.O. had to think about it. "Jacobs, I'm pretty sure. Yeah, that's right, Jacobs."

Kolchak said the man's name as if it left a taste in his

mouth, and out of the corner of Keller's eyes, he saw the officer crinkle his nose with disdain. A partial grin formed over Keller's lips. "Jacobs. That makes for an easy night's work. Glad it's him."

"Yeah, he's all right, I s'pose." Kolchak didn't sound too sure.

Keller hated Jacobs. It was as simple as that, and when he was working up his plan for tonight, it was Jacobs who he hoped would be assigned to the shift. The guy was smug, arrogant, and a complete asshole all the way around. One time, when he checked in during the night, Keller was doing paperwork at the desk. Jacobs snuck up behind him and shouted, right next to his ear, 'Up against the wall and drop your scrub pants, pretty boy!' It startled the hell out of Keller. He jumped up swinging, thinking it was an inmate from the block units, and he wasn't about to be turned out. That wasn't the case, though.

It had been Jacobs. He caught Keller's swinging arms and proceeded to beat him about the stomach with his stick. Keller doubled-up, a puking mess in a ball on the floor. The bully stood over him laughing, telling him it was all in fun and to keep his murdering mouth shut. He said that Keller better buck up, because this was how things were done in night laundry. He made sure to tell him again that it was all in fun. Then he left Keller in his vomit, laughing all the way out the door to the laundry sally port.

Yes, Jacobs would do; Jacobs would do just fine.

"Well, Keller, here we are."

Kolchak waved to the guard in the Reception & Delivery control center.

The door buzzed, and Keller entered ahead of the officer. Turning around, he thanked the man standing at the door, who also bid him goodnight. Then, Keller turned to the inmate he was relieving. The guy held two softcover paperbacks in his hands. Two books, and not a lot of laundry, Keller thought sarcastically. The inmate left without so much as a spit to his feet.

"Good riddance."

Making his way to the desk, he checked the daily logs. Keller found himself thinking about Jacobs. The man would be by any second to do his first check. Keller planned to wait until after the midnight supply delivery to act. Once the boxes of supplies were secured in the area, Jacobs would take a final look around, and then Keller would make his move.

Picking up his clipboard to see what the other prisoner had or hadn't done, Keller began going about his night as if everything were normal. He even hummed to himself as he stood with his rear end propped against the edge of the big oak desk, facing the sally port and the corrections officer entrance next to it. Any second, that jerk Jacobs would come through the door, spouting his nonsense, and Keller would react as he always did, with a smirk and a nod, or a 'yes sir,' if the situation warranted.

Keller would continue to perform his duties over the next few hours, but soon enough, his behavior would take a drastic turn.

Right on time, the officers' entrance door buzzed loudly. Jacobs slammed his way inside, and Keller could immediately tell that the man was irritated. Snow and cold air rushed in around him. He had a sneer on his face, and he appeared to be a bit flushed, a look that didn't complement his bright-red hair.

"Keller! I see you're going at it. Good! I don't want any hassles tonight. If I get any, you can kiss this job goodbye. I have my own problems to worry about without having to worry about you too."

Jacobs stood in the doorway, letting the cold air and large flakes of snow blow inside. Keller stood still, clipboard in hand and page half-turned. The only thing he had moved since the man presented himself were his eyes, and now they held the officer's mean gaze.

"Well?" Jacobs was beginning to raise his voice.

"Yes, sir."

The prison guard flinched slightly at the stillness in Keller's voice and the lack of reaction to the man's words. Feeling a little uneasy, Jacobs glanced over his shoulder at the watchtower outside, then stepped through the door and let it slam shut behind him. Strolling over to Keller, he stopped before him and put his face directly in front of the inmate's as he narrowed his eyes. It was his full intention to provoke the convict. Keller set the clipboard on the desk, intent on keeping eyes with the bully of a correctional officer that stood before him. Maybe he wouldn't be waiting until two after all. This guy was going to jack up his plans if he wasn't careful, and he wasn't about to let that happen.

Suddenly, the intercom buzzed to life, surprising both men who were now on edge.

"The soap and toiletries delivery is here!"

Jacobs jerked his head to the right. "Now?"

"Yep. Early because of the storm coming!"

"Pop the sally! Let's get this over with!" Jacobs said, after a brief pause. He turned back to Keller and smiled. "Aren't you the lucky one?"

"I suppose I am, sir." Keller stared.

Jacobs' smile faltered once again, then he muttered in a low voice, "Let's get it done."

Keller made the guy nervous; he knew it. He also knew it was the reason that the young ginger-haired punk treated him like he did. Sure, the guard was rude to the others, but Jacobs was a special kind of menace when it came to Keller. It was almost as if he would tie up and torture Keller if given the opportunity. Keller would love to give him a chance because he'd flip the script on the punk so fast that he'd find himself in a very painful alternate universe.

Keller tolerated the insolent man the best he could for the next hour while unloading toiletry boxes. Jacobs held the clipboard, making sure the order had been adequately filled while the truck driver sat in the cab of the truck. He was a lazy loser, and though he put on good appearances doing the bare minimum, he was just below a bonbon-eating fatty who was addicted to *As the World Turns*.

As Keller analyzed the two men and their weaknesses, he realized it was time to act.

"Wait, I put the wrong number of boxes of toilet paper here," Jacobs said. "You said fifteen hundred-count boxes, right, Keller?"

"Fifteen, right." He pretended to recount with a pointed finger, but his eyes were on Jacobs' back. Keller was well aware this distraction would give him the time he needed.

Jacobs turned his back on Keller to set the clipboard on the desk to erase and correct. He left his oversized black flashlight on the desk chair, forgotten while doing the task. It was perfect. If Keller had one thing going for him, it was the speed at which he was able to think and move.

Keller snatched up the flashlight so fast that his movements were nothing more than a blur and a shadow. With a single powerful overhand swing, he smashed Jacobs in the head with the large end of it. The man instantly crumpled to the floor, lifeless but for a few random twitches here and there. Keller looked down at him with a smile before repeatedly smashing him in the head. Blood was pooling all over the concrete floor beneath him, threatening to hypnotize Keller and distract him from the goal. If he had more time, he would have sodomized the loser right then and there with the flashlight.

At last, Keller stood back, swept his long, sweaty black hair from his eyes, and smiled down at the man again. His head was nothing more than a bloody pulp with a small spot of brain pulsating grotesquely from his frontal lobe. The pulses were visibly slowing down, and Keller was tempted to sit and watch until they stopped altogether. But there was no time to take pride in his work. He ran over to the truck's rear that was still sticking through the sally port. He kicked the back.

"Hey, we need you in here!" he yelled to the driver. "These orders are all messed up, man!"

There was no response, but he heard the man get out of the truck and slam the door. In seconds, the entrance was popping open, and the driver was coming inside. Keller, who was hidden just inside, waited for the door to slam. As it did, he hustled the driver against the wall, forcefully gesturing the flashlight towards the guy's head.

"Take off your clothes," he growled.

The driver began to whimper. "Don't... please. I have– " The driver's eyes widened when he saw the dead guard.

"Shut up and take off your clothes!" Keller gestured meaningfully with the flashlight.

Seeing no other option, the man shed everything

except his underwear. He was shivering from both the cold and his fear. He tossed the items on top of a box of toilet paper, just as Keller directed him. Turning to the convict expectantly, he waited for his following instructions, but there were none. Keller smiled at him, pushed him against the wall, and smashed the flashlight into his head. The man dropped to his knees, then instantly fell over dead. Keller looked him over; there were no pulsating bits of the brain this time. Boring, he thought.

It was time to dress. First, he pulled his hair back into a makeshift bun using a rubber band from the desk drawer. If anything gave him away, it would be his long black hair. Next, he put on the driver's uniform, including his hat, ensuring any stragglers from his black tresses were tucked up inside. He had given himself a good shave that day, and in the dim lighting, he doubted that the guard tower would see his face. He was cautiously optimistic the control center guard wouldn't recognize him. He'd be out of there in less than ten minutes.

Keller lowered the door on the back of the truck, secured it, and pressed the button as he exited. "It's just Justin, the driver," he said into the box after they answered him. "They thought they were short on TP, but we got it all straightened out. Inmate can't count for shit."

Without suspicion or further scrutiny, the door

buzzed. Keller stepped out into the snowstorm and went around to the truck's driver's side, jumped in, and pulled out. The timing couldn't be better, the storm threatening to whiteout. He watched as the corrections officer lowered the sally port door from the Reception & Delivery control center in his rearview mirror. Keller smiled, nodded, and gave a partial salute to the guard as he passed by and drove through the checkpoint. The officer didn't even bother to open his window, not wanting to risk letting out all the heat from the tiny guard shack.

The road was snow-covered, and his visibility was low. Keller was delighted. In less than ten minutes, he drove down the highway, leaving a trail through the freshly falling snow, away from the prison and out of sight.

FIVE

T he lobby door burst open, sending snowflakes into the air. A cold breeze could be felt across the room. "Hey, babe! I got the broken heater in that second cabin up and running like a top. You might want to get in there and freshen it up. You never know what'll happen with this second storm going on." Rick closed the door and continued stomping his feet to get the snow off his boots.

Donna looked up at Rick from the very last of the file work she had been pounding away at. It took her a full two weeks to scan the remaining historical files from the cabin resort into the new system, making sure they were all in properly labeled folders and somewhat discernible order. The project consisted of so much work that they wondered if it was worth it. What were the odds that they would ever put the files to use? They hoped they could easily extract a few names for future promotions without shifting from one box to another. Maybe it was worth it. Plus, if there was ever a fire, everything was now somewhere in a cloud in cyberspace, never to be lost. Yes, it was smart.

"I'm on my last stack here," she said, beaming as her husband removed his coat and headed for the coffee pot. "When I'm finished, I'll get to cabin two. I doubt anyone will be rolling in demanding that specific cabin. We have others we could rent while I get that one spruced up. Sometimes you think the goofiest thoughts, I swear."

Rick rubbed his hands together, then grabbed the carafe of coffee and poured a steaming hot cup. "That's fine. By the time you take your little butt over there, the cabin will be nice and warm. It smells musty, though, so I figure you'll want to dust and change the linens and towels. I don't think we've rented it out in a while, have we?"

"No. I'll give it a good going over. Now, let me finish this." Donna went back to the files, and Rick, who had managed to drain the last cup of coffee, set about making another pot. The couple worked quietly. The only sound was the scanning of old paperwork and the percolation of the coffee pot. Rick stood before it like an impatient child who just had a bubble gum machine steal all his change. His fingers tapped impatiently against the counter as the chills from the frigid outside air continued to course uncomfortably through his body. He was also tapping his foot, as though the extra movement would intimidate the ancient coffeemaker and make it speed up.

"This has got to be the slowest pot in the free world," he muttered. "You know, my love, if things pick up, even in the slightest this year, our lobby and the full continental breakfast will be going through an overhaul before the new season begins. New coffee pot, some furniture that doesn't look like it came out of the Bates Motel, and maybe even an expansion, a kitchen, so we can begin to serve meals on grounds."

"It may seem slow to your impatient self, but it spits out a pot in just a few minutes. But, okay, I'll concede: if things pick up, we'll get a brand new one just to make you happy," Donna replied with a shake of her head.

"I like where you're going with this!" He grinned with a sparkle in his eye.

The resort was spectacular and worthy of their respect. It sat on its little private point of land, with a sparkling blue lake and nothing but dense forest behind. On the hill, in the far distance, they could see the town they planned to hike to someday. It was stunning, the twinkling lights at night, the patches of dark green dramatically lit.

Finishing the very last of the files, Donna returned them to the old box from which they came, then stood, stretched, and made her way to her coat. She grabbed the key to cabin two, tucked it into her pocket, and made her way to the laundry and supply room. They had just refinished it, and everything was stacked nice and neat. There was a section for housecleaning supplies, one for sheets and linens, and one for soaps and toiletries. Donna loaded a housekeeping cart with everything she needed to spiff up the cabin, pecked her husband on the cheek, and made her way out of the office, across the lot, and to cabin two. Thankful Rick kept up with plowing, she was able to push through the snow quickly enough.

Rick took Donna's seat behind the desk. It was the best seat in the house, enabling anyone who sat behind it to see all who entered and exited from the lot. There was also property access from the lake in the back, but it would be near-impossible to reach the small beaches directly behind the resort itself at this point in the winter storm. It would take a special kind of man to endure the frigid, deadly waters at this point in the game. So, Rick kept his eyes on the office doors, windows, and parking lot.

THE MAN STEPPED OUT FROM A DENSE THICKET of bushes. He was wearing a brown delivery suit, and his face was partially covered with a ski mask. It was colder than sin out there, but he was pretty sure he had found a safe haven where he would be comfortable until the storm eased up. Then he could continue his route to

Rocky Mount. There was nothing like traveling to make one's heart full.

He approached the cluster of cabins. He was starving, exhausted, and his feet hurt something awful. He could see a pretty woman pushing a cart across the parking lot through the distance. A man about the same age was sitting near a big picture window.

Yes, this was more than perfect.

Something got Rick's attention out of the corner of his eye: a man in what appeared to be a brown delivery suit entered the lot, and he was on foot. He looked to have a thick black scarf covering the lower part of his face which looked matted with ice and snow, at least from what he could see from inside the office. He also wore what appeared to be a delivery man's hat. It, too, was matted with a pile of snow. Rick rose and made his way to the door to open it for the stranger. Hopefully, the man wanted a cabin, but if nothing else, Rick could at least bring him inside and warm him up with a stout cup of java. Surely, he would appreciate that. He couldn't imagine where the man had come from.

As soon as the door opened, a frigid gust of air rushed in, blowing melted snow and ice behind it. The man quickly entered, and Rick closed the door behind him. More than curious, he turned to give him a good once over, trying to read him by his outward appearance. Rick got a strange vibe from the visitor that was more than off-putting; it was uncomfortable. The guy hadn't yet said a word, so what was all this apprehension about?

"What seems to be the problem, sir?" He asked politely. "Do you need to rent a cabin? Did your vehicle break down or get stuck somewhere?"

The passer-through shivered violently and shook his head in response to both questions. "Umm, could I please just have a cup of coffee for now, please? I sort of need to get my wits about me, you know. It's so cold out there I could barely breathe."

Rick jumped into action. "Oh, yeah, man. Sure thing. Do you take it black?"

"As the night," the man replied.

As Rick poured the shivering man a large cup of coffee, his curiosity nagged at him, and he repeated his question. "Did your vehicle break down somewhere down the main road? I mean, not to impose, but if that's the case, we have a dependable winter tow service here in Thompson Trails that would be more than willing to help you. The sheriff has a tow plow, and he takes great pleasure in putting that beast to use."

He handed the coffee to the stranger, who still hadn't removed the partial ski mask he was wearing. It wasn't a scarf after all, and it was covering most of his face, except for his eyes. He sipped the coffee right through the slit in his mask, sopping it with the hot liquid. Rick supposed he didn't mind the intrusion, as odd as it was. He hoped the hot coffee would warm his lips before he hit the road once again if it didn't sear the flesh from it first.

"So, you rent these cabins out, huh?" the man asked as he looked around.

Rick leaned against the main desk with his elbow and sipped his coffee. "Yeah, but I have to admit, we weren't expecting any guests during this particular storm. We had a doozy of a storm two weeks ago." Rick suddenly got the overwhelming feeling that this was the last man in the world he wanted to rent to and hoped he didn't ask for a cabin.

The man held his black eyes on Rick's hazel ones, never shifting his gaze. He stared at him as if he was reading the innermost parts of his mind, delving into his most personal thoughts. A chill came over the young resort owner, and he tried, unsuccessfully, to shake it off. This shiver had nothing to do with the weather. This stranger was off, and the heebie-jeebies he was sending in Rick's direction made him queasy and defensive at the same time. The more time Rick Welk stood with the drifter in the lobby of the Virginia Trailhead Cabins, the more he wanted to crawl out of there and run screaming. He glanced at Donna's empty chair and was glad she was in the cabin.

"So, Mister -" he began.

The outsider smirked. "Derringer. Elias Derringer."

"So, Mr. Derringer, were you interested in one of the

cabins for the week?" Rick anxiously waited for the words, 'no.' One guy's money wasn't going to make or break them in the slightest.

Derringer took a long slug of the slowly cooling coffee while taking note of the security cameras. "I'm not quite sure. They look pretty quaint, but I'd rather get a look at one if you don't mind." He dreaded being on camera and always kept an eye out for them.

"Well, you head on outside. My wife is cleaning one, so I'll grab my coat and meet you out there so you can see what we have to offer." With that, Rick went into the men's room, and Elias Derringer wasted no time leaving the resort lobby and heading to the cabin with a cart parked in front of it: cabin two.

Rick stood at the head, draining his bladder. His mind reeled about the stranger. What was his name? Derringer. Elias Derringer. Something wasn't right about the man, something that Rick couldn't quite put his finger on. While seemingly pleasant enough, the guy had shifty eyes and a weird disposition. Rick was feeling even sicker to his stomach. Had he just sent that stranger ahead of him to cabin two, alone, while his wife was the only one in there? Rick's hands were trembling, and he felt an acute sense of urgency. Rick needed to join his wife to make sure that all was well. Had living here made him too trusting? Something inside scolded him for being so stupid. He felt like he had just done one of the dumbest things ever in his life.

He rushed from the bathroom, grabbed his coat, and ran out the office door. Derringer was nowhere in sight, so he figured he was already in the cabin with Donna. The entrance to cabin two was slightly ajar, and the lights from inside were casting a wedge of illumination over the snow. Now and then, he could see the shadow of either Donna or the visitor as it passed through the light stream. Rick picked up his step and started a slow jog through the rapidly piling snow on the lot.

As Rick approached, he could hear Derringer speaking to Donna. "So, I see it's pretty dead right now," he was saying. "Is that because of the weather, or are y'all dead around here most of the time, pretty lady?"

Donna chuckled, but the nervousness in her voice was telling. "Um, just the storm, I'm pretty sure. We're busy most all the time." She paused. "Where did you say my husband is?"

"Oh, just using the facilities, ma'am." The man laughed, but there was something a bit sinister to the sound. "You must get pretty lonely out here, what, with your husband leaving all the hard stuff to you." The outsider shifted his weight from one leg to another to relieve the pressure on his toes.

"No, he does all the hard work," she replied pleasantly, burying her concern and nervousness. "I just pick up the slack around here and handle the paperwork."

Rick picked up on the shift in the man's voice. It was

flirty, but there was also an undertone of dirtiness. As though the thoughts in his mind weren't matching the concern that he was feigning. He felt the overwhelming need to get this guy off the property. Rick took hold of the cabin door, swung it open, and planted a tight-lipped smile on his face.

"So, Mr. Derringer... what do you think of the cabin?" he asked. His voice bordered on rude now. He didn't want Elias Derringer renting a cabin or anything else for that matter. The guy's aura was filthy, and its blackness was almost something he could see and touch.

Both Donna and the stranger were startled by his sudden emergence, though he noted that his wife looked relieved to see him. Derringer, on the other hand, looked more amused than anything. Rick's belly gave another uneasy lurch. Was this guy playing games, or was Rick over-reacting, as Donna often said he did?

Derringer smirked. "Not bad. Not bad at all. As a matter of fact, pretty cozy, considering all things. You two have sure managed to make a nice little getaway spot here for passers-through, I have to say." The man looked at Donna and gave her a wink. Her face turned red and even a little green around the gills. The guest was managing to make her very uncomfortable indeed. She turned away from him and went into the bathroom with a can of cleanser and a toilet brush.

"So," Rick continued, his eyes still on his wife

protectively. "Are you interested in renting or not?" His smile was tight, and his hospitality had reached its end.

Derringer began to pace around the cabin once again, poking his head into the bathroom, the small closet, and even kneeling to look under the bed. He examined all the windows latches and door locks for weakness. Derringer contemplated overpowering Rick, but he felt exhausted and weak from the long trek in the cold. More importantly, Derringer wanted something to eat and a weapon. "How much for the night?"

Rick wanted to laugh. "We just rent by the week. After all, these are Virginia Trailhead Cabins; most guests make a time of it. It's not a roadside inn, you know. A week is two-fifty, full facility access, including canoes, lake use, and ice fishing."

"You aren't willing to rent to me for a single night?" Derringer asked, an edge to his voice. "Even with the storm and all? I mean, I ran into some bad luck in Donneley's Pass; got robbed, you know. Could use a shower and a place to lay my head."

Rick shook his head. "Sorry, man. We're not very flexible. A week only." He didn't want the so-and-so there for another second.

Out of the blue, Derringer broke out into a sick, dangerous laugh, as though Rick had just cracked the funniest joke of all time. Both Donna and Rick stared at him as the laughter ran its course, glancing at each other uneasily out of the corner of their eyes, half-smiles on their faces to appear polite.

"Nah, I think I'll have to pass. These are a little too rich for my taste, ya see. And how would I canoe during this storm?" Derringer said and belted out another laugh.

Rick nodded. "Well, I'm sorry to hear that, Mr...."

"Derringer," the man replied through gritted teeth, with a sneer and a glare in Rick's direction.

Rick nodded pleasantly and smiled with relief. "Yes, Derringer. My apologies. Well, as you can see, the missus and I have to finish cleaning and get moving with other chores. You know, if you head right on the main highway, the town is a mile up the road. The sheriff's office is about on the right, and old Sheriff Brown and his deputy are always more than willing to help out. He even hands out vouchers to travelers in need to stay at the local hotel up in the next town, probably will drive you there too. That would be your best bet. If you want, I'll give him a call for you, and I'm sure he'll pick you up and take you himself."

Derringer's eyes perked up. The town was only a mile away. His taste buds were watering for someplace to eat. He maintained his odd grin and continued to look around the cabin covetously. "Nah. I'll hike, I do believe. Thompson Trails is a pretty small homestead. I think I'll be just fine. Well, now, folks. Thank you for the hospitality, but I do believe I'll be on my way."

The nerves in Rick's body started to relax. "Well, sure

was nice to meet you. Hope you don't hit the worst of the storm that's coming."

Derringer stopped at the door and turned back to both of them, offering Donna one more wink. "Oh, I do believe we're still in for the worst of the storm that's coming, Mr. Welk. The worst of it, in the worst kind of way."

Derringer left cabin two slamming the door shut behind him. When Rick peeked out the flowered curtains, he saw Derringer heading for the entrance to the lot, and he let out a deep breath.

"What a weirdo," he muttered.

Donna went back to changing the sheets on the bed. "Well, I don't know, dear. Everyone is weird in their own way. He seemed pleasant enough to me."

"The look on your face said differently," he replied in disbelief. "I saw your eyes, and I know you heard how he spoke and acted. Something is wrong with that guy."

She shrugged and ignored him. It didn't matter; the stranger was gone now. His odd behavior was no longer a concern for Rick and Donna Welk.

CHAPTER

SIX

The snow, even though the flakes were huge and falling gracefully, was coming down in great torrents. The wind blew ferociously, whistling as it spread across the region. The six o'clock evening news warned all residents and travelers to seek and take shelter immediately. It didn't look as though this one was going to pass anytime soon. It felt like it was never going to end.

Well, this is the way it goes the uncertainty, the pain, and the doubt, all of it. The weather was frigid, and the icy gusts of wind made it even worse. Derringer kept his head down against its onslaught. He trudged through the rapidly piling snow and thought about the couple back at the cabin resort. Derringer could tell that the husband was leery of him. Odds are, Rick had no idea that he was a mass murderer, but Derringer could tell by the look in the man's eyes that Rick was very uncomfortable in his presence, as he should be.

Derringer considered taking Donna Welk and showing her a trick or two while they talked in the cabin. To his obliviousness, Derringer didn't hear a word the lovely blonde said to him, not a one. He was too busy wondering what her blood would feel like dripping from his fingers or how she felt from the inside with his brutal fist. But then, alas, the mister came charging across the lot with a whole different attitude than the gracious and hospitable man Derringer met in the lobby. He was as cold as the air itself.

Derringer fought against the elements, then paused briefly to adjust his foot, still in the delivery guy's boots. It was pretty uncomfortable, not to mention they were a size too small. He had left the delivery truck when he sent it careening down the side of a steep embankment, about three miles back. There was nothing better than amusing entertainment with a cute girl, especially when it came to the fun and games he liked to have with the female species. It was his full intent to indulge himself, but he needed some food and rest right now.

His mind went back to the Welks. Yes, he would return there, and he would have his fun. He would christen every cabin at that resort with the blood of that couple, and he would stretch out his recreation for as long as possible. He was prepared to be caught but hoped he could play his games and move on to many more. As for right now, he was starved. He wanted some warm food. There must be a café open around here, he thought.

He was sure there had to be an all-points bulletin out on him all over the state of Virginia and the surrounding states as well.

Derringer's appearance made him stand out in a crowd. His long, scraggly black hair was a dead giveaway. He made sure it was tucked out of sight under the hat, and he figured he would be safe from capture, for a while anyway. He wouldn't go easy. When the time came, and he was at risk for being captured, he'd kill anyone threatening his little adventure.

Derringer was more than halfway to the town when he crested the hill. He noticed a small metal building off to the side of the road. It appeared to be an old, abandoned feed store. From his vantage point and a glance around, he could see the whole town. The streets were deserted nothing, but a few scant streetlights shone. He ducked and crouched down behind the building to get a reprieve from the wind. Defeated, there was no diner or fast-food joint insight. He decided to wait here until the sun went completely down, then he would make his way back to the cabin resort. The Welks should be in bed by then. He was frozen and drained. He figured he could find a way inside one of the cabins, warm up, and wait to take that pretty petite blonde by the throat the following day at the first opportunity.

An hour later, Derringer crossed the parking lot at the Virginia Trailhead Cabins. Cabin ten had the flicker of a television light shining through the drawn curtains. That must be the Welks' quarters, he thought to himself. Making his way to the front of the office, he crouched down next to a snow-covered garbage can and tried to get warm once again. He was shivering like a leaf in a high wind, his toes numb, and he was starting to feel like he was coming down with something. The urge to cough was overwhelming.

He couldn't hold back any longer, no matter how hard he tried. Derringer lost control. He began to hack and choke in earnest. His body was so wracked with the coughs that he didn't see or hear Rick Welk open the door to the cabin and look out at him. Derringer continued to hack and cough, unknowingly.

Rick felt a little shiver of anxiety, then kind of an unpleasant chill. "What are you doing back here?" Rick's voice startled the escapee.

Derringer swung his head, trying to think fast while trying his hardest to stop the choking. He felt fury build up inside of him at the self-righteous prick standing there, looking at him as if he were a pile of dog crap that hadn't been cleaned up. Keller was in no condition to overpower Rick.

"Um, I'm sorry, sir," he said, trying to sound as cold and miserable as possible. "I just needed to warm up, just for a second. I lost my direction, and I think I got turned around in the storm. Is it possible I could do some work for you to get a cabin for the night? Help you shovel or something?"

Rick stared at him, his stomach giving a lurch of warning. He thought about the request considering himself out in the cold like this man was. He would offer the same for shelter. But Rick had to base his decision solely on his gut instinct, not on empathy when it came to Derringer. Rick had always been one to follow his senses, and he wasn't about to deviate from that habit now.

"Look, man, I'm sorry," he replied, trying to be kind but with an edge to his voice. "You simply need to go. I'm sure if you head to the sheriff's station, he'll put you up for the night." Rick's gut tightened another notch.

Derringer sneered. "You think so, huh?" He contemplated going back to the feed store for shelter and rest.

Rick stared at the man, knowing something was off, so he backed up into the cabin and closed the door, leaving only a crack. "Yeah. Just turn right on the highway, and it's about a mile up on the right."

"Heck," Derringer muttered as he stood and headed to the abandoned building. He'd be back. This guy better know it.

Rick watched him walk away until he was out of sight on the highway, then he closed the cabin door and locked it. A light breeze rustled the curtains. "I'm calling

Sheriff Brown. That same drifter was out there under the awning next to the garbage can. Maybe they can find a nice warm place for him in jail."

Donna was standing in the middle of the room, looking pensive and far away. "But he hasn't done anything wrong, has he?" Donna asked, but also wondered about the stranger. He wasn't so innocent-looking, and why would he be wandering about the way he was?

Rick shook his head adamantly and picked up the phone. "I don't care if he's the son of Mother Teresa; I'm calling Bob."

Donna didn't argue and watched while Rick dialed Bob's office. He filled him in on the vagrant and how uncomfortable the guy made him feel. Bob reassured Rick that he would head out right away and track down the guy, then told him to hit the hay, keep warm, and sleep well.

Feeling relieved, Rick did just as his friend suggested, and in no time at all, he and Donna were both snoring lightly, all thoughts of the odd man pushed aside for the night.

SHERIFF BOB BROWN SAT BUNDLED UP IN THE pickup plow, a magnetic cop light on the dashboard turned to the off position, with the heater and defrost set to high. He was parked facing the direction of the cabin resort, waiting for any sign of the vagrant Rick had reported, and as he watched, he hummed along to a country song telling him how mama had tried to raise him better. He wished that the guy would show his face. Bob wanted to get home to his sweet Rose and some warm apple pie.

It didn't take long for the man to appear, even in the near-blizzard conditions. The tall shadow of the man could be seen struggling through the snow as he made his way toward the sheriff. The drifting snow was causing him to stagger a bit, and the high winds didn't help matters. Bob noticed that he was wearing a partial face mask, probably his best clothing choice of the day, all things considered. But why was this man out wandering around in such conditions?

Bob watched, his eyes squinted in the darkness, as he reached for the spotlight on his car door. He ran through all possibilities first, wondering if he were homeless or mentally ill. He was worried the spotlight would freak him out and send him into some kind of tizzy. Instead, Bob turned on the fog lamps to not blind the man, then slowly began to drive in the stranger's direction. The snow was accumulating fast, he observed. Everyone would be using their snowmobiles by morning. He was thankful at the moment that he had invested in this great big rig.

Bob inched along at a snail's pace, taking note that

the man didn't slow or stop at his approach. He continued to walk at an even pace in the calf-high snow. His hands were in his pockets, and his head was covered with a hat. The sheriff pulled up next to the man, stopped the truck, and rolled down the side window.

"Excuse me," he hollered to the traveler. "I'm the sheriff here in Thompson Trails. Is there any way I can help you?"

Bob squinted at him in the darkness, looking for any reaction or response, but the guy acted like he didn't hear or see him. Sure, the wind was blowing fiercely, Bob thought, but he was practically on top of the guy, any closer and he would run him over. The sheriff waited for a response, but the guy continued to walk.

Bob cleared his throat and shouted. "Excuse me! I'm Sheriff Bob Brown. Could I have your attention, please?" That got a response, and the man stopped dead in his tracks. He kept his head down, not turning around, and his hands were still buried in his pockets. Bob clucked his tongue, shook his head, and put the vehicle in park, rolling up the side window as he went. Why did all the strange so-and-so's in the world have to make every single thing so complicated?

Bob unclipped his gun at his side and got out of the truck, hand securely on his pistol. Slowly, he walked around to the back, where the man was standing at the bumper of the truck. The Sheriff approached him slowly, his hand still on his revolver.

"It's mighty cold out here," he said kindly. "You have to be about frozen by now. Is there anything I can do to help you?"

When he received no reply, he continued. "Boy, you came to town at the wrong time. Nobody's really taking boarders, you know. I guess you must've tried down at the cabins, but even they've decided to shut in for the night." He paused again. Now it was Bob's turn to feel uneasy. The guy didn't act like anyone who needed help, despite the danger. He'd seen a few unstable ones in his day, and this one was up there.

"I'm going to have to ask you for some identification, please." Bob tightened his grip on his gun.

Finally, the stranger turned in his direction and offered a pleasant smile. Bob could only identify it through the eyeholes of the half-mask.

"I ain't got none, sir. See, that's the problem: I was robbed down at Donneley's Pass at the truck stop. All my money, license, everything—gone. I was just trying to make my way as far as I could 'til I finally got home safe."

"Where you from?" Bob began to relax a little, his story sounding legitimate. Maybe it was just the darkness and the wind that made the man seem eerie.

The visitor took a deep breath. "Rocky Mount."

Bob took a good look around. The streets were completely dead and snow-covered. It was ridiculous and inhumane to leave this guy standing out in the middle of the storm. The least he could do was let the guy warm up and help him figure something out. It was his duty.

"Hey, if you wanna climb in the truck, we'll get you warmed up, run your name and all. Make sure you're clear. If you're good to go, why, we'll just put you up in our one-cell pokey for the night, free of charge. Then, in the morning, we can call down to the train station in Donneley's Pass, get you a ticket, and I can run you on the snowmobile to catch the train to Rocky Mount. How's that sound to you?"

Derringer thought about it for a fraction of a second. "Sounds wonderful to me. I can't thank you enough."

The two men were seated in the pickup plow, contrary to state law and local policy. Derringer had his gloves off and rubbed his hands together in front of the heater vent. Bob poured the man a steaming cup of coffee from his thermos, then used an old Styrofoam cup for himself. Grabbing his notebook and pen, the cop decided to get down to business.

"I'll need your name, date of birth, and social security number, please."

The man gave a shiver as the heat began to settle into his bones. "Derringer. Elias Derringer. Birthdate, June sixth of sixty-nine."

Bob scratched at the notepad furiously. "Social?"

Derringer smiled on the inside. He had thought of this before and used the name, Elias Derringer, as well as the man's birthdate and social security number on several occasions, all successfully. Elias was his cousin on his mother's side. He was locked up in a private institution, all expenses paid by his wealthy mother, safe from the public eye and all scrutiny. The idiot had never been in trouble a day in his life; he could barely wipe his own bum.

More scribbling, Bob took the handset to his police radio and called into the station. "Hey, Darren."

"Go ahead, Sheriff."

"I got this half-frozen man with me. I need you to run his information right quick."

"Ok, I'm ready," a younger voice replied.

Bob gave the information over the radio, then refilled their coffee cups. "So, you're from Rocky Mount, eh?"

"Yeah, but I'm just 'Passing Through.' I ain't had an opportunity to come out here in a while. Most of my relatives are fairly well-off; they live in Roanoke. But I have some old friends I stop in and see in the Mount. Why?" Derringer looked out of the corner of his eye at the cop. "You know anyone from there?"

"Nah. Thompson Trails folk are born here, they live here, and mostly they die here too. The only time I ever leave is to take the wife to her doctor appointments at the Pass." Both men chuckled at that one.

The radio crackled loudly, "Sheriff?"

"Ya, go ahead."

"Sorry, it looks like the lines are down to the State. I've tried a few times, and the page won't load. Oh, wait,

Sheriff, it is loading. Says here Mr. Derringer's clean as a whistle."

"Oh, good. Thank you, Darren," the Sheriff replied. "Seems he had a touch of trouble down in Donneley's Pass; got robbed but good. We're going to put him in the cell for the night and, in the morning, we'll get him a ticket to Rocky Mount out of the town fund. Why don't you go ahead and get it ready?"

"Will do."

With the radio conversation over, Bob turned to Derringer. "So, you ready to get a warm shower and some sleep? We don't have much food, maybe a couple of microwave burritos in the fridge, and I think there might be a donut or two. I hope that will do."

Derringer smiled slyly to himself. "That would be just perfect, sir. Once again, I can't thank you enough."

As they whipped a u-turn to head back to the station, Derringer thought, "Oh, but I'm sure I'll find a way to repay your kindness, Sheriff Brown."

SEVEN

"Howdy, Sheriff!" Deputy Darren Rush's voice seemed to boom inside the small main office in the brick building that served as Thompson Trails city hall and jail. The man was young, no more than twenty-five, and he had a bright red jarhead haircut that seemed to stand straight up. Derringer could tell he was tall and thin, even though the kid was sitting down with his legs under the desk. Probably six-two, but he couldn't have weighed much more than a buck-eighty.

Sheriff Brown grunted. "Howdy. Smells good in here. Bet this was the first real cleaning this place has had in a year." Knowing Darren just wiped down the rubber mattress with cleaning spray. He turned to Derringer. "In case you hadn't guessed already, we don't get many overnighters here in Thompson Trails, at least not in the jail. Mostly, it's here for appearance's sake." The sheriff gave a big belly laugh at his own joke.

Darren stood and held out his hand to Derringer. "I'm Deputy Rush; nice to make your acquaintance. You can call me Darren if you like."

"Likewise. I'm Elias. Elias Derringer."

Rush gestured around the musty, dusty room, which had two desks piled high with files, leaving just enough room for feet to rest. "I know it ain't much, but the shower works, and the blankets are warm."

Derringer forced a pleasant smile. "Much obliged."

Darren fetched a neatly folded towel, washcloth, toothbrush, and bar of soap. "Ain't got no paste, sorry. The shower is right around the corner when you're ready. Oh, and I put a pair of clean blue scrubs inside for you to sleep in."

"Thank you."

Derringer gave them a nod and headed to the shower area while Bob plopped down and gave his own feet a rest. Removing his glasses, he began to polish the condensation off them, his mind on his wife, Rose. Bob knew she was okay, safe at home in the storm, but he always kept her in the forefront of his mind. Bob was responsible for the pretty little lady, after all. She was his dream girl and the love of his life.

"You ain't heard from my Rose, have ya?" Bob asked.

Darren sat back down. "She called about fifteen minutes ago. She's going to bed, and your meatloaf is in the oven. Oh, yeah, she said there's a big ole slice of pie in there too."

"Good, because I absolutely want that." The two men laughed hard at that one.

Rush cleared his throat. "So, you feeling okay about this stranger, are ya?"

Bob snorted. "Why shouldn't I? Poor guy got robbed, and he's been struggling all the way from Donneley's Pass. He'd have to be one hell of a psycho to pick tonight to do any damage. The guy's harmless."

"I'll take your word for it," Rush replied. "There's hot coffee there and a couple of donuts leftover from supper that the missus bought. Otherwise, I think there might be one more beef and bean burrito in the fridge. Want me to heat it for him?"

"Perfect," Bob replied, putting his glasses back on his face. "But find out what he wants first; can't be wasting food. I'll hang out for a bit, have a word with Mr. Derringer and get to know him a bit. But guess what?"

Darren groaned. "Don't tell me. I'll be staying overnight with him, just to keep an eye on our guest."

"Precisely."

The two men began chitchatting about the recent storms, comparing them to the last big one the town had seen, five-years prior. Thompson Trails ended up stacking this snowstorm on top of a small one they had only two weeks ago. According to both of their recollections, the big one from five years back had nothing on this one. This one was being touted as a killer by journalists and meteorologists.

Derringer rounded the corner. He was wearing the blue scrub pants and shirt, which appeared to be a size too large for him. His towel was draped loosely over his head, and in his arms, he carried the clothing he had been wearing. It was neatly folded, with his boots on top. His wet hair was pulled back into a loose ponytail.

Bob jumped up. "Oh, here you go, Mr. Derringer. Let me take care of that for you." The man grabbed the dirty laundry, boots and all, and walked them over to Deputy Rush. Derringer thought about the gun he had tucked in his holster. It made him smile.

"Darren here is going to be pulling night duty tonight since you'll be staying over and all. He'll need to keep himself busy, and this is a good way for him to do that, maybe catch up on some paperwork. Besides, got to stay in practice for when real criminals come to town, wouldn't you say, Darren?"

The deputy laughed sarcastically as Bob put the neat stack of belongings on the corner of his desk. Deputy Rush grabbed the boots and put them on the floor next. Then he picked up the dirty clothing and stood to his feet.

"Oh, yes, sir," he replied. "As a matter of fact, there's no time like the present. Maybe you'd see fit to hook this man up with a bite and some coffee. I'll be back." He turned his head in Derringer's direction, "I will put your stuff in the wash."

Rush went down a small hallway and out of sight while Bob waved at the donuts and coffee. "We also have those burritos I was telling you about, Mr. Derringer."

Without answering, Derringer poured a cup of straight black coffee and grabbed a glazed donut. He thought how easy it would be to take the gun from Deputy Gomer Pyle. With the other hand, he popped a burrito into the microwave. Derringer took a single bite of the donut, turned to the sheriff, and leaned back against the table holding the refreshments. Obviously, the kid is gullible. He would wait till the sheriff left and get the pistol from Deputy Gilligan. As he chewed, he stared the lawman in the eye, observing his every move. His eyes were nothing more than narrow slits. Then he would make his way back to the cabin and hold them at gunpoint. He would enjoy some of that tasty Donna Welk. He was always thinking ahead, even more so since escaping from prison. It was best to anticipate anything from anybody, especially two cops.

Bob stared back at him in silence, the smile he was wearing on his face disappearing in slow motion. Derringer was a creeper, all right. No wonder Rick Welk didn't want to deal with the guy, money or not. Most of the locals, including the Welks, would've put someone up for free in weather like this, but for some reason, Rick had refused, and that wasn't like him. As Derringer took another large bite of his donut, Bob was pretty sure he understood why. Unexpectedly, he wanted to get out of there and fast, but he wanted the stranger locked safely in the cell first.

"Sorry to tell you, but per state and county policy, we'll have to keep the cell locked tonight while you sleep," Bob quickly explained, faking a brand-new smile. "You know, it's more for your safety than anything, what, with all the weapons. Plus, you never know when some dangerous criminal will come in here and pull something crazy. I'd sure hate to see you get hurt in a situation like that."

"Dangerous criminals coming to Thompson Trails," Derringer muttered around his donut bite. "No, we wouldn't want that now, would we."

Bob chuckled nervously just as Rush came around the corner. "Well, they're all in the wash for you. By tomorrow, they'll be nice and fresh, Mr. Derringer."

The man gave him nothing more than a nod in response, then shoved the last of his burrito in his mouth all at once. Draining his coffee, Derringer wiped his mouth with the back of his hand and gave a cockeyed grin.

"I suppose I'm pretty beat," he said, giving an exaggerated stretch and yawn. "All that hiking and trudging through the snow, and then those punks at the Pass. I'll bet I'm gonna sleep like the dead."

Bob jumped to his feet, grabbing some magazines

and a few random books. He handed them to the man before opening the cell and letting him in. When the door was securely locked behind Derringer, who made himself comfortable, Bob turned to Rush.

"I need you to fetch me the files," he said, giving a sly wink to his deputy.

At first, Darren looked confused, but he quickly straightened up. "Oh, yeah. You wouldn't believe where I found those files earlier today in the female inmate folder. Come on, let's get them. Are you going to take them home and write up some new ones? You know, those Richmond cops called earlier complaining about that again."

"Yep," Bob replied, all business. "That's my plan."

As the two cops walked out of the room, Derringer pretended to thumb through the books. He watched them out of the corner of his eye. They weren't on to him. The phone hadn't rung, and there was no fax in the machine. No, he just made the sheriff nervous. That was all. Derringer made everyone nervous. It was one of his favorite traits; he wouldn't want it any other way. He decided on the book, *Brother's Keeper,* as he made himself comfortable, mumbling quietly. "This book sounds terrific."

Captain Russell Johnson of the State Patrol enjoyed his first day off in months. He had just finished stoking the fireplace and was pulling out his seat at the dinner table. He was about to have dinner with his lovely wife. Sue Johnson was busy in the kitchen, and the smell of pot roast filled the air. He was ravenous, "you know hon," he hollered to her. "I'm excited to have these few days off. I hope we get snowed in. I sure do need this break."

Sue rounded the corner smiling, holding two plates of food. She set the meal on the table, and he planted a long-awaited kiss on her lips. "I can't agree with you more. I hope you're hungry. I made you extra gravy." She said with a wink.

No sooner did she sit down when his cell phone chirped. "Son of a–." He put his hand to his face and leaned back. He was running his fingers through his thinning hair and scratching the back of his head. "Now what? I can't even have a full day off more or less enjoy dinner." He answered, "Captain Johnson."

It was Detective Jack Fowler, "Sorry to bother you at home and on your day off, but we're in a world of shit. I think you would have wanted me to call either way." The edge to the man's voice was noticeable. "It's nuts here. I figured I better call you. A call came in this morning from Virginia Max."

Johnson immediately sat forward in his seat, "what happened."

"Keller escaped. We had to launch a nationwide manhunt."

For the life of him, Johnson couldn't believe what he was hearing. He spent six months making sure this psycho was locked uptight, and they threw away the key. Now all of a sudden, Keller was loose on the street. His head was spinning. His stomach turned as he recalled the horrendous scenes, the visions of the three girls haunting his memories.

"I'm not sure how we're going to get the APB out. The fax line has been down all day, and IT is trying to get the internet back up. Thankfully, we still have phones," Fowler stated, the exhaustion in his voice tangible.

With extreme trepidation, Johnson continued, "How did he escape maximum security?" Sue's eyes perked up hearing the conversation Johnson was having.

"Apparently, he worked the night shift, he killed the guard, and a delivery driver then stole the delivery truck. It happened last night around midnight. They found the two bodies this morning during the 6 am shift change."

Johnson was astonished. "We'll need to call and notify everyone via phone manually. I'm on my way." Johnson hung up the phone and filled his wife in on the awful details. I take one day off the entire state falls apart.

When Johnson walked into that cabin over five years ago, it changed his life. To this day, images of the butchered teen girls flash in his mind. He wouldn't sleep until this madman was behind bars again. Soon he was on his way to the precinct.

"WHAT FILE ARE YOU TALKING ABOUT? YOU'RE not making a lick of sense!"

Bob and Darren were standing in the back-file room, waving dust around to keep it out of their faces. Darren had already sneezed more than once, so the sheriff was trying to be patient, waiting for him to get it together.

"It's nothing big," he said. "The guy just gave me a bit of the creeps. I'm ready to go home. Look, I know the state cleared him, but be on alert and practice the strictest of procedures, okay? You never know who you got in a place like this. More than likely, it's nothing more than he's told us. Just cold, tired, and hungry, and I can say the same for myself."

"Got it," Darren said as he sniffled into a hankie.

Bob continued. "Now, first thing in the morning, I'll call and buy him a train ticket to Rocky Mount myself. Then, you take him, most likely by snowmobile, to catch the train in Donneley's Pass. Maybe he'll even spot those thugs who ripped him off. That's the plan. I want this guy out of Thompson Trails before my gut proves me right, just like it always does."

Bob gave a firm slap to Darren's shoulder, smiled grimly, and continued. "Not that I think anything's going to happen, mind you. More than likely, the storm has me all paranoid and up in arms. All I'm saying is exercise precaution; he's a stranger in these parts. Clean record or not, we always need to keep on the side of caution, son. Don't be overly suspicious with him or rude, but don't get too close, either. I mean, who ventures out on foot in this weather when they get mugged? No one that I've ever seen."

Darren nodded soberly. "Yes, sir. Anything you say."

"All right." Bob grabbed an empty file folder, tucked a couple of blank sheets of printer paper inside for good measure, and the two left the room.

Together, the two officers made their way back out into the main office. Bob filled Derringer in on the plan for the morning, including details about buying him a ticket to catch the train in Donneley's Pass. Darren's wife, Avery, would be bringing him a nice breakfast first. Bob also reassured the man that he would cover the ticket's cost and that Derringer didn't have to worry about money.

With everything organized and planned to a tee, Sheriff Bob Brown left the station with a heavy heart and a knit brow. The guy's odd but pleasant enough. He thought as he climbed into his truck and started it up. As he rocked the truck back and forth to get it out of a building snowdrift, he realized why his chest was so heavy. The guy was ungrateful. They were bending over backwards for the man, and he hadn't even thanked him for the price of the train ticket he'd be buying. Heck, he didn't even say goodnight when Bob left the station. And the man's eyes seemed to look right through him, as if he were reading his thoughts or trying hard to, anyway. Yes, something was off, all right.

Bob would feel better when the man got on the train in the morning and as far away from Thompson Trails as possible.

EIGHT

"Well, here we are," Darren said in a friendly voice after he closed and secured the door of the building. He plopped down at his desk and put his feet up. "Hope you got your belly full. If not, I can still heat another burrito for you."

"I'm good," Derringer said as he turned another page in the book.

Darren began to twiddle his thumbs. The silence was awkward and loud, especially in the company of a guy who was very guarded and distant. People like that always made Darren nervous. He was an extrovert to the core, and without conversation, he practically crawled out of his skin. Darren started looking around for the new book he wanted to read. He knew it was around here somewhere. Darren just ordered it. It was delivered just a few days ago. He loved reading small-town psycho thrillers. That's when he noticed the book in the visitor's hands. He was reading it. Bummed out, Darren could at least tell the man was enjoying his brand-new novel. He had no choice but to grab an old magazine that Bob kept around for laughs and began to flip through it for the millionth time in his career, but soon he was bored with that as well. He needed to pass the time.

After about an hour, Darren broke the silence. "So, what do you do, Mr. Derringer?" he asked, unable to help himself.

The guest sighed and put his finger on the corner of the page he was about to flip. "I'm a personal delivery consultant."

Darren was thrilled that the man responded to his question, so he put his feet on the floor and leaned forward. "Really? That sounds cool! Better than police work, especially in this podunk town. So, what does a personal delivery consultant do?" he asked sheepishly.

Derringer gave a short chuckle and shook his head at the cop's childlike inquisition. "Well, let's see. I, um, consult. With people. People I deliver things to."

Darren nodded and smiled as if it were as clear as a bell to him. Seconds later, he realized the depth of sarcasm and belittlement behind the description, and his cheeks flushed red. Darren looked down at his hands, which he started to twiddle once again, albeit subconsciously.

After a minute, the deputy stood. "I think I'm gonna watch a little television, if you don't mind."

"Actually, I do." Derringer put the book down, stood up, and crossed the cell, stopping at the bars and grasping them with his hands. "I mean, I'm just so exhausted, and I have a pounding headache. I think that's why I was kind of short with you; sorry about that. Anyway, I'd just really love to get some sleep."

Darren breathed a sigh of relief. The guy wasn't a jerk after all. He just didn't feel good. How could he, after his day? "No problem. I get it. I'll just dim the lights in here, keep my desk lamp on, and tinker around. Don't mind me. Oh, and if you need anything, anything at all, don't hesitate to ask."

"Thanks," he replied, backing toward his bunk. "I'm gonna go to sleep now."

The deputy nodded one last time. "Have a good rest, sir."

Derringer didn't respond. He simply turned his back to the man, hiked his wool blanket over his shoulder, and began to doze off.

Darren sat there trying not to obsess over his new book locked in the cell. He didn't have the nerve to interrupt the man and ask him for it. He just sat there bothered and bored, with a sad look on his face.

12:14 A.M.

Derringer snored lightly in his cell, seemingly sleeping like a baby. He was right, Darren thought. When the guy said he was exhausted, he meant it. There hadn't been so much as a peep from him since the last words they had spoken.

Darren was bored out of his mind and twice as exhausted. So far, the deputy drank two full pots of coffee, and a third was in the process of brewing. He was pacing quietly around the office area trying to stay awake. He couldn't play games on his cell phone because the reception was non-existent, and shuffling cards quietly while someone was sleeping was no easy task. Yes, indeed, coffee was the only thing that could save him now.

As if on cue, the pot stopped churning, and Darren quickly made his way to it, cup in hand. He had just picked up the hot pot and was getting ready to pour when the phone rang. It wasn't a loud ring, really no more than a light series of chirps, but it startled him, nonetheless. Who could that be at this time of night? It had to be the Sheriff, or someone was in the middle of a major snowstorm emergency.

Gingerly, Darren put down the pot and cup, then tiptoed to the phone as fast as he could. On his way by, he looked in at Derringer. It seemed like he hadn't moved a muscle. Plus, Darren could still hear his faint snoring. The phone hadn't rousted him in the least.

"Sheriff's Office, Deputy Rush speaking," he

answered in a low voice. He knew Sheriff Brown was worried, but calling this late was ridiculous. He'd reassure him right away and get him off the phone.

But it wasn't Bob. "Deputy Rush, this is Captain Russell Johnson of the State Patrol. Hope you're having a good night up there in the middle of that snowstorm."

"Well, sir, it's pretty bad, but here in Thompson Trails, we tend to stay in and wait it out. It makes for strong family ties if you know what I mean."

The captain chuckled at the joke, then Darren continued. "How can I help you tonight, sir? Hope it isn't anything too bad, considering the hour."

There was a pause on the line. "Well, we can hope not, not for you boys, anyway, since most of the cable and internet lines are down across the region. It's hard to know who has service and who doesn't. We're forced to telephone other law enforcement agencies to make them aware of an active all-points bulletin that is currently in effect. See, we've had a prison convict escape from Virginia Max in the last twenty-four hours. And he's extremely dangerous."

Darren hadn't received a call like this since he got his badge. While it was a bit exciting, catching an escapee in Thompson Trails wasn't something he could see happening. Not right now. He would hear the guy out, document the report, and thank him kindly.

"Who would this be, sir?" he asked.

Johnson cleared his throat. "I'm sure you've heard of Elliot Keller?"

Rush's heart skipped a beat. Of course, he'd heard of Elliot Keller. The guy was sick as hell. Darren shuddered, just thinking about what he did to those girls and that boy in the cabin.

"He-he's the one?"

"I'm afraid so. Anyway, we have the APB out, but we're having a hard time getting photos out due to downed lines." Johnson paused. "If you have a notebook, I can give you a description."

Darren quickly sat at his desk and grabbed a pen. "Shoot."

"White, six-foot-two, approximately one-hundred eighty-five pounds. Long, scraggly black hair, countless tattoos. Keller did have a thick goatee at the time of the escape, but we suspect he shaved it off. Also, two men were killed during the escape, a correctional officer at Virginia Max and a delivery driver who was dropping off a load of supplies at the prison. Keller made away with the delivery truck; even dressed in the guy's uniform and danced right through the gate."

Darren didn't hear most of the last couple of sentences. He was staring into the dimly lit cell, merely ten feet in front of him. Panic began overwhelming the young deputy. The captain just described the visitor to a tee. Thankfully, the man was still sleeping soundly, light snore and all. His back was to Darren, and it still appeared he was trapped in the throes of his dreams.

"Deputy? Did you hear what I said?" Johnson's words snapped him out of it, but he kept his eyes on Derringer and lowered his voice another notch.

"I think I can help you with that, Captain."

Another pause, then Johnson replied quietly. "Do you have the inmate, Deputy?"

"Well, I'm not sure, but I believe we do." Darren waited, heart pounding, for Johnson to say something, anything, that wouldn't force a conclusive answer from him, a response that might give this inside information away. Would it matter if he did hear the conversation? He was in a cell, after all. The thought of being trapped in the locked jailhouse with a mentally unbalanced mass murderer in the middle of a blizzard didn't appeal to the young deputy.

Johnson was puzzled by his roundabout replies. "It sounds like you're not able to talk right now. Is he listening?" Johnson asked.

Darren was relieved. "Yes, sir, that is correct. I'm sure that the Sheriff and I will work something out in the future. We often transport prisoners from other counties, but the snow right now makes it virtually impossible. I'm sorry to hear about your housing problem, though." He tried to make small talk and was failing miserably. Hopefully, the captain would understand his subtle hints.

"I understand," Johnson said. "As much as we'd love to, we simply can't take him off your hands right now. We need you to hold him until the weather lets up and the roads clear. Are you able to do that? Is he contained now?"

Darren gave a fake chuckle. "Absolutely. It won't be a problem to continue working it out."

"I'm going to get ahold of the Department of Corrections," Johnson continued. "In the morning, I'll call back to discuss the situation with your sheriff. In the meantime, keep your distance. This is a serious situation. That man must remain securely behind those bars, Deputy Rush. Be sure to let your sheriff know immediately. We'll be in touch."

"Will do," Darren replied cheerfully. "Hopefully, we can help you out when the snow clears. You have a good night."

Darren hung up the receiver and sat back. Derringer or was it, Keller? Still hadn't moved, as a matter of fact, his snoring seemed more profound. Darren tried to remain calm and think. His first step was to call the sheriff, and he had to be slick about it.

Quietly, he picked up the receiver and started punching numbers. The sheriff's line rang twice, then crackled and went dead. Panicked, Darren hung up to try again, but there was no dial tone. Talking to Bob would have to wait until morning.

Only five-and-a-half hours from now.

KELLER WASN'T SLEEPING. KELLER WAS WIDE awake, listening to the one-sided conversation from the cell. His fake snoring was effective, as it always was when incarcerated. But he knew exactly what that call was about, and he knew that there would be no riding with Sheriff Brown to Donneley's Pass. No, he would have to make it alone, but before he did that, he had a mess to clean up by the name of Darren Rush.

He heard Darren dial the phone and could tell the calls weren't going through. What perfect luck! The lines had gone down. Now, he could go ahead and deal with the issue at hand before anyone else became wiser.

Darren Rush would be easy. He was an inexperienced moron. It took Keller seconds to plan out his escape. Now, all he had to do was wait for the perfect opportunity to put it into action.

It wouldn't take long at all with this idiot in charge.

NINE

D arren sat silently behind the desk for the next twenty minutes, coffee forgotten, staring at Derringer's back as he slept. In his mind, getting the news to the sheriff about their guest could wait until tomorrow, but his stomach was telling him something very different. Darren had a persistent nagging feeling that he needed to get Bob on the phone as soon as possible. He didn't like being the only one with this kind of information. The man was a ruthless killer. It was unnerving, to say the least. It wasn't as though they could do anything about the situation tonight, but he didn't want to be alone with a guy like this, even if there were iron bars between them.

Carefully, the deputy fished his cell phone from the hip pocket of his uniform pants. He glanced with a grimace. All he had was a single signal bar. He might be able to slip a call through to Bob's cell. He pushed the send button with high hopes, but the 'call failed' flashed on the screen immediately. Checking the landline one more time, Darren held the receiver to his ear. He heard nothing and replaced it gently in the cradle. As quietly as a mouse, he stood up and crossed the room, then down the small hall to the laundry area. He could pretend to be putting Derringer's clothing in the dryer while he tried Bob again.

Once he had the clothes going, he checked his phone and saw that the bar was gone. Walking around the small room, holding the device in the air, proved fruitless. Frustrated, he placed it back in his pocket and stood frozen. Darren's anxiety, combined with too much coffee, was making him extremely jittery. He had never dealt with a seriously hardened criminal, let alone this complete animal. The grim reality was that he was stuck hanging out with this guy until morning, whether he liked it or not. He had to find a way to cope with it and accept it. He reminded himself that the man was behind bars. Everything would be fine.

He sure hoped that Bob got there before his wife Avery showed up with breakfast. He didn't want her anywhere near the monster. Darren was half-tempted to hang out in the laundry area until morning. He didn't trust his own instincts, and even he knew he could be naïve. What if the man took him for a ride or tricked him? His mind was playing out horrible scenarios. No, he couldn't hide; he was a cop! He had to buck up and go out there and do his job.

As he began walking back down the hall toward the front office, he heard the sound. It was a deep, guttural gurgling that sounded about as unearthly as anything he had ever heard. Picking up the pace, Darren sped out front just in time to see Mr. Derringer lying on the floor of his cell doing the floppy fish. He was having a seizure. It was severe enough that Darren feared the man could swallow his tongue. He was starting to foam and drool. His eyes were rolling back in his head, and his back was arched stiff. His left leg was thrashing about. At first, Darren watched, his mind racing for answers. He decided to take a leap of faith, not wanting to watch a man die, even though he probably deserved it. All reason left him, and he headed for the cell, keys in hand.

"Hang in there!" Fumbling for the proper key, Darren stood at the cell door. "I'm coming. Don't you die on me!"

Locating the key, he put it into the lock and turned it. Once in, Darren dropped to his knees beside the twitching, seizing Derringer, and tried to steady the man's head. He searched aimlessly for something to put in his mouth to bite down on.

"It's going to be okay," he said as his eyes scanned the cell. "It's going to be fine." Darren grabbed his brand-new book and shoved it into Derringer's mouth, instructing him to bite down.

Immediately, Derringer's seizure stopped. The book fell from his mouth with teeth marks embedded into the spine and cover.

Confused, Darren looked at the man to find him staring up at him and smiling. "Don't you think a night in the hoosegow is much more fun when somebody dies?"

Darren arched an eyebrow, his mind unable to grasp what was happening. One second, the guy was seizing. The next, he was talking about good times in jail. Darren's mind was reeling and his hands were shaking. Cold fear slowly began to coarse through his veins. He knew he'd been had, and the dread in his stomach was replaced by the harsh acceptance of his impending death.

Keller's arm moved swiftly. But, as if in slow motion, Darren watched the scene unfold out of the corner of his eye. The man had his gun, and it was pointed dead at the center of Darren's chest, the barrel pressing painfully against his skin. His eyes shot back to Keller, and he shook his head helplessly.

"No... please my wife."

"Don't you worry, Deputy Rush," Keller sneered. "I'll be sure to have plenty of fun with her too."

The firearm went off with a loud bang, and the air was filled with the smell of gunpowder. Blood and bits of flesh were everywhere, including all over Keller. He kept hold of the deputy's dead, but still upright, body and looked him over with intrigue. Keller knew he would never tire of watching the life drain out of the eyes of another human being. It was one of the most exciting things on Earth for Keller to witness. There was no power like it. Keller could go without food for weeks, if they would just let him kill a couple of people a day.

Finally, he tired of watching and let the dead man flop over. He stood and grabbed the deputy's feet, then dragged him to the small mop closet down the hall near the shower and laundry area. He covered him with a couple of spare wool blankets. Keller undid one of the deputy's boots and tried it on. He wiggled his toes and thought *good enough*, then removed the last boot. Next, he mopped up the floor but wasn't aiming for perfection. The blood wouldn't be apparent right away if someone decided to stop in. He figured it would buy him some time. They would look in and see the jail empty and the deputy absent. The small, missed spots of blood wouldn't matter once he was gone. Not until the dead deputy's wife brought breakfast. Oh, how he was tempted to wait for that little honey. He hadn't had a good piece in a long time.

Keller began to rummage through the other closets and found several police uniforms and hats. He chose a uniform that was just the right size, then showered and got dressed. Keller was ready to roll. He took the deputy's keys and wallet, then left the building, locking it securely behind him.

As soon as he stepped outside, he turned around and

smiled. Look! How convenient was this? Deputy Dumbass parked his truck right in front of the building, as though he wanted to make things as easy on Keller as possible. It was covered in snow, but that wouldn't be a problem. The white stuff was light and fluffy, and it would take no more than a swish or two of the wipers and a couple of scrapes to clear things up.

As he climbed inside and started the ignition, he thought now was a good time to drop the whole 'Derringer' routine. It was just a temporary ruse, after all. Everyone knew that he was Elliot Keller. Best to keep it that way. Besides, he had come to hate that name, knowing what kind of man the real Derringer was, pathetic and weak. Well, it just didn't fit.

Keller struggled to control the large vehicle, pulling away slowly through the drifting snow. The roads were covered from the snowfall. The wind had brought drifts the likes of which he had rarely seen. He had to weave around fallen branches and downed lines. Keller was just getting to the town limits when he hit a patch of ice under the snow. The truck went into a deep skid. The vehicle slid off the road, down into a ditch, and slammed hard into a massive oak tree.

The airbags deployed, keeping Keller's head from bouncing off the steering wheel. But he was left stunned and dizzy. The left side of his head bounced off the driver's side window, creating a gash. It was gushing plenty of blood. He sat there, breathing in and out, trying to let it all sink in and evaluate how badly he was injured. After about fifteen minutes, he took the keys from the ignition and got out of the truck. One look around told him everything he needed to know. He was in the middle of a blizzard, and the closest place for him to seek shelter and keep from freezing to death was back to the jail. Keller was going to have to get his head on perfectly straight, figure things out, and work with this situation as best he could when he got back.

He felt a warm trickle on his temple running down his face, so he reached up and touched the spot. He looked at his hand. He got knocked around in the accident. So much for the effectiveness of airbags. Keller walked back to the driver's side door and reached inside to turn the headlamps off. No need to draw attention before he could figure things out. Keller would leave the truck right where it was, and it would be completely buried by morning. His one regret was that he hadn't put Rush's body in the truck before leaving. Had he thought of that, they wouldn't have found him until spring. The thought made him laugh.

He began to stagger off, back in the direction of the jail. He stayed off the main road as much as he could, walking to the side in the deep drifts. He was freezing, but his mind was on too many other things to let it get to him. Keller was busy thinking about the gun he still had in his pocket, the deputy's he had escaped with from Jail. The fact that they hadn't recognized him was nothing short of a miracle, though Keller adamantly refused to believe in miracles. In order for there to be a miracle, there had to be a god, and there was no such being in Keller's reality. No, this was just sheer incompetence. Anyway, he still had the handgun, and it still had some bullets in it, so no matter what happened after he returned, he would have his own back easily enough. Besides, when he returned to the jail, he could take a plethora of other weapons, along with ammo. He would be set up but good.

The high drifts and winds slowed his travel. It took Keller more than forty-five minutes to return to the jail. The walking released pent-up adrenaline, which was helpful to get under control. He hadn't passed a single car, nor light on, from the residences as he walked by. The town was dead, which calmed him. He sure never expected to find refuge in jail when he escaped. The irony made him chuckle out loud. Soon enough, he'd be back in that warm bunk in a clean pair of scrubs, and whoever happened to pop in next would be none the wiser. Not only wouldn't they know what transpired between him and the deputy, but they'd be oblivious to the phone call he got from the State Patrol.

At last, he reached the sheriff's office. He fumbled with the keys briefly, then let himself back inside, locking it behind him. Turning up the lights, he noticed a couple of blood spots he missed on the floor. So, the first thing he did was grab the mop and take some extra time to get it all. Next, he went to the back and changed out of the police uniform and into a fresh pair of prisoner scrubs. He tucked Deputy Rush's wallet into his underwear, the safest place he could think of at that moment. Bagging up the uniform and bloody mop head, he went out the back door and threw them into the dumpster, then came back inside to warm up again. He also took some ammo from the guy's desk and took it all back into the cell.

Dimming the lights, Keller took the deputy's keys and locked himself back inside the cell. He hid the keys and gun under the fire-retardant plastic mattress he'd be sleeping on. Keller tucked himself in and let out a long, tired sigh. He needed some actual sleep, and it wasn't going to take long to get it. Not even the mystery of who he'd have to deal with next was enough to keep him awake. His biggest concern was the arrival of the State Patrol, but he had time to figure out a plan before they came to take him back. He had enough ammunition to keep them at bay long enough to take a few with him. Now was the time to get some sleep.

The last thing that ran through Elliot Keller's mind before he passed out was that he wished he had heard the entirety of the phone conversation between the deputy and the State Patrol. That would've enabled him to plan much more efficiently. He knew they were going to be coming, but it certainly wouldn't be this early. No one in this part of the state was going anywhere tonight, but they would arrive to fetch him soon enough.

But for now, it was time to rest up because he was most definitely going to need it.

KELLER HAD A DREAM.

He was in the basement. It had a door but no windows like in an ordinary house. The distinct smell of evil was prominent—the wet, moldy, stinky basement with his damp, smelly blanket. There was a rat in the corner, and it was taunting him with its squealing. Sometimes, it would come out and nip at his little boy toes, but when he screamed, it would run back into the shadows.

The cellar was different this time. It didn't have a rotting wooden door like it always had. Instead, it had bars. Keller looked down at his body, and in the slivers of light that came through, he could see he was wearing striped jail clothes, like on TV. He thought they looked clean, which was strange. His parents never gave him clean clothes, not for as long as he could remember.

"Hey, boy! Are you feeling a bit hungry? Or are you just bored?"

His father's voice brought panic, and he chose not to answer. If he answered, he was always wrong, so little Elliot learned to keep his mouth shut. But in this dream, he could tell that his father wasn't alone. He was dragging someone down the stairs with him, and the person was struggling.

Suddenly, the lights came on, blinding him and causing him to cover his eyes. When he opened them, he saw his father standing there with a smile on his face. He was holding his mother, bound with rope, tightly by the arm. She had duct tape over her mouth, and she was crying heavily. In his other hand, his father held what appeared to be a single cookie. They had been his favorite, and his mouth began to water.

His father threw his mother hard to the dirt floor, her head bouncing off it. She lay limp and crying as her husband unlocked the cell door. He waved the cookie at his son.

"Do you want the cookie, Elliot? If you do, you have to let me do one thing."

Elliot nodded eagerly, his stomach screaming for the tiny bit of food.

The man set the cookie on one of the crossbars of the cell door. "Now, don't you try to grab it! You just lay there and let me do what I gotta do, and when I'm done, you can eat that cookie, okay, Elliot?"

He nodded again.

His father reached into his pocket and pulled out two small safety pins. Then he approached the minor child. He laid him on the wet mattress and straddled him, pinning his arms beneath his knees.

"Now, Elliot, this will hurt for a second, but it will feel good for a lifetime."

His father, his daddy, began to put the pins through his eyelids and forehead skin, pinning his eyes open so he couldn't blink or close them without horrific pain. He sat the boy up and propped him against the rotten concrete wall.

"Now, you watch how I teach your mother a lesson, and you can have your cookie."

For the next hour, Elliot Keller watched his father do the most unspeakable things to his mother that could be imagined. Not only did it tear his heart and mind apart, but he lost the will to live in that moment. His father kicked his mother around until she was unconscious when it was over. Next, he removed the safety pins, took the cookie from the bar, and looked at his bleeding son.

"Did you like that?"

Elliot nodded, his mouth watering for the cookie.

"Good. Because I like cookies."

The man popped the entire cookie into his own mouth, locked the cell, grabbed Elliot's mother, and went back upstairs. Elliot cried until he passed out from the anguish.

ELLIOT WOKE, FURIOUS AND SHAKING. IT MAY have been a dream, but it was based on reality. It had happened to him over and over until Elliot Keller finally killed both of his parents and buried them under the dirt in the basement. He was fifteen. He became a ward of the state because he was considered a 'deserted youth.'

Yes, all of that was horrific and painful, but his father made him the man he is today.

TEN

B y five o'clock the next morning, the snow in Thompson Trails showed absolutely no signs of letting up. In fact, it was falling like mad, as if there were an avalanche coming straight down from heaven. The entire region was in a State of Emergency. No one was to venture out in their vehicles to try and brave the roads for any reason. If travel was necessary, it was advised to use snowmobiles. Fortunately, most townsfolk had them, but most wouldn't be using them that day.

Avery stood in the kitchen of the small, cozy home she shared with her husband, Darren. She was packing an insulated cooler with plates of hot breakfast food wrapped in foil: eggs, bacon, pancakes, and hash browns. Avery also had two water bottles filled with cold milk, silverware, and napkins. She zipped the cooler shut and walked over to the window to get a look outside. Shaking her head, Avery put on her heavy parka and thought how miserable the snowmobile ride would be on the way to the station. Fortunately, she started the contraption shortly before, so it would be raring to go by the time she was ready to head out.

Avery wrapped her scarf tightly around her face and neck, then donned a thick woolen cap before pulling her parka hood over it all. Next, she put on her insulated gloves, grabbed the cooler, and headed out the door, neglecting to lock it behind her. After all, no one in Thompson Trails ever really locked their doors. Mostly just the banks or other such businesses. Crime just wasn't a problem in those parts. After securing the cooler with bungee cords, Avery hopped on the snowmobile and aimed the vehicle through the snow drifts towards the sheriff's office.

Her thoughts along the way were light and carefree. The snow was overwhelming, but man, was it beautiful. Even as it fell, it rested on the branches of the trees like lace. It reminded her of a snow globe, and she planned to take pictures when the storm passed because it was as pretty as a postcard. She smiled beneath her scarf and thought about how happy she had been since marrying Darren. Everything was working out for her according to plan.

Avery hadn't told him yet. She was saving the news for his birthday, which was right around the corner. It's a boy! She was simply beside herself with joy. Even though Darren was a man, and he often withheld emotions or feelings that weren't 'manly,' she knew he would be just as excited as she was. Even now, as she rode the snowmobile around the corner to the sheriff's office, she swore that she could feel the little life growing inside of her. But it was too soon for that, Avery knew. After all, she was just over two months along. She couldn't wait to feel kicks.

The first thing Avery noticed as she neared the station was that Darren's truck was gone. She was confused; wasn't he supposed to be staying all night because of the drifter? Surely, there was a good explanation, so she pushed her concern from her mind. Perhaps Bob had to borrow Darren's truck. It was Thompson Trails, after all. Nothing surprised her when it came to the simple workings of this small town.

Avery slowed the snowmobile and pulled it next to the space that should've been occupied by her husband's truck. There was much less snow drifting in the area, so she figured that either Darren or Bob, whoever had the vehicle, would be able to maneuver back into that spot reasonably easy when they returned. For now, she needed to get the food inside.

She left the vehicle running and released the cooler from the bungee cords. Stopping long enough to fish the station keys from her parka pocket, she headed up to the door and let herself in. The lighting inside was still dim, the way they kept it when they had inmates, which wasn't very often. The usually musty-smelling station was exuding the metallic smell of stale pennies, something Avery had never caught in the air here before. She stopped and looked around the room before reaching to her right and adjusting the lighting tone. The office was empty, and now she could smell a combination of bleach and pennies. Very strange. Avery's eyes darted to the cell where the guest was soundly sleeping, locked in the cell, with his back to her. She could hear his light snoring.

"Ex-excuse me," she uttered timidly. "Hello, sir?"

The man squirmed and moaned, then appeared to settle right back to sleep. Avery's eyes were scanning the station. Where was Darren? Where was Sheriff Bob?

"Darren? Honey? I'm here with breakfast." Maybe he was in the restroom. She knew her husband, and he was definitely in the restroom first thing in the morning.

Her words managed to rouse the man in the cell, however. He suddenly turned over and made eye contact with her. A smile quickly grew over his face, and his black eyes seemed to pierce her cornflower blues. Avery shivered and fought the temptation to yell louder for her husband.

"Well, hello, pretty lady," the man said as he swung his feet to the floor. "You must be the deputy's missus." He wouldn't let this opportunity go to waste, looking her up and down.

Avery smiled shyly, but her eyes continued to scan the room rapidly, and she listened intently for any sound that signified she wasn't alone with this stranger.

"Yes, I am," she replied in a soft tone. "I brought breakfast for you two men. Where's Deputy Rush?"

The man gave a chuckle, stood, and gave a long, leisurely stretch as though he had just woken up. But he had been wide awake for hours. "I'm not sure. I think something happened with Sheriff Bob's snowmobile, and he went to help him get it started or something. He said he'd be back shortly. I think he's been gone for about a half-hour. How're the streets out there, anyway? Any sign of things clearing up?"

Avery relaxed and placed the cooler on Darren's desk and proceeded to open it, getting the breakfast items ready. "No, not really. As a matter of fact, I expect the storm to last at least two more days. It's crazy. Even the plows won't be able to hit the roads until then. It's the worst storm I've seen since I was a kid." Avery let out a nervous laugh.

Keller listened politely, entertained by her edgy nervousness. As he watched her trembling hands and anxious disposition, he was amused. It tickled him that his presence put her on edge. That was the exact sort of thing that turned him on the most.

Avery took up his plate, bottle of milk, and silverware wrapped in a napkin and made her way to his cell. "I'm not exactly sure how to get this in there to you," she said with a smile. "Usually, one of the men is here to take care of that."

Keller took two short steps to the cell door, grabbed a couple of the bars, and smiled out at her alluringly. "No worries, pretty lady. Deputy Rush left the keys to the cell with me. He said you might be here before he gets back." Keller dangled them outward in her direction. "See? Here they are."

Avery stared at him, her smile fake but her nerves alarmingly real. "Um... would you please unlock the door? There isn't any way for me to get this into you unless you do."

The man continued to look at her with his eerie smile. He was dangling the keys persistently as if he were trying to hypnotize her with them. Why did he look so familiar to her? There was something about him, something inside of her was trying to drum up a reason why she may have seen him somewhere before. It hadn't been a good recollection, whatever it was.

Keller chose a key on the ring. He paused, looking up at her right before reaching through the bars to put the key in the hole. "So, have you talked to Sheriff Brown? I assume he'll be heading down here soon? I'm ready to get on the road to Rocky Mount, and he's supposed to be buying me a ticket and sending me on my way."

"I haven't spoken to him, but if he said that's what he's going to do, you could count on it happening."

She turned to offer him a nervous smile, but she

didn't have time. In a snap, Keller grabbed Avery in a bear hug. He squeezed her so tight she could neither breathe nor scream. She began to kick her legs frantically, her heels coming into hard contact with his knees and shins, but the blows didn't faze Keller at all. The twisted man simply began to laugh, amused by the entire confrontation.

He flung her to the floor, where Avery began to cough and scramble to get away from him. He watched her for a moment, entertained, as she gasped for air. She was crawling, and she was under duress. Then he chased her, grabbed her by the ankles, and dragged her backward until they were by the deputy's desk. Her piercing screams echoed in the building.

"I say we have a little fun before we eat our breakfast," he offered. "Might as well take advantage of all of this alone time."

"Please, don't," she sobbed. "I'm pregnant!"

Keller laughed hard. "Oh, goody! Two little birds with one giant stone!" Her piercing screams grew louder.

Keller lifted her and flung her down hard on top of the deputy's desk, knocking the wind from her lungs. As she lay there struggling to breathe, Keller began to tear at her snowsuit, throwing each piece here and there as it was shed. Finally, after all the struggling, he removed her jeans. He put his hands on her shoulders and leaned over into her face. Keller was looking her in the eyes and smiling.

"Now for a little fun," he sneered.

Unexpectedly, Avery's arm swung forward and around. Keller felt a sharp sting down the length of his right arm, and a surprised look came over his face. She had a letter opener in her hand, and blood was oozing from his fresh wound and running down her wrist.

"Oh, you want to play?"

Keller grabbed her by the shoulders and shook her hard, like a rag doll. Her head slammed off the desk, stunning her. Taking advantage, he grabbed her by her neck and squeezed till she was blue. Avery passed out, and the child inside of her would soon be his youngest victim.

Keller stopped and put his hand to his arm, then looked at the blood on his hand. You little, he thought. Oh well. Either way, she was going to die that day. There was nothing she could've done to save her own life. With a smile, Keller proceeded to have his way with her body, right there on her husband's desk. The event seemed to last forever, her breathing was ragged, and her eyes were about to flicker open. The sight, sounds, and smells were perfect, bringing Keller's dreams to fruition. Avery's eyes flashed open to see his body jolt to a climatic finish. The traumatic vision of horror would haunt her soul for eternity.

When Keller was done, he grabbed her by the head, twisted hard one time, and snapped her neck. Without an ounce of compassion, he looked her over one last time.

In the corner of his eye, Keller could see the blood flow from his arm with every heartbeat. He was losing blood quickly and needed to tend to his wound.

Keller locked the station door and walked back to the restroom area to look at his bloody arm in the mirror. The wound was long and gaping, but the very sight of it made him smile. Avery has done an excellent job with nothing but a letter opener for a weapon. He thought about finding a sewing kit and trying to stitch it up, but he had two reasons not to: the sheriff would be there soon, for one, and secondly, he liked how it looked. It added to his natural good looks.

Leaving the bathroom, Keller peeked outside the window. The woman's snowmobile was there, still running, but he didn't want to risk taking it when the sheriff was due any minute. No, Keller was going to tuck himself away with his gun behind the station door, and there he'd wait patiently for Johnny Law to come in and find the mess he made. Then, and only then, would Keller wrap up the little party he was having at the Sheriff's Office. After that, he had other business to attend to in Thompson Trails: unfinished business.

With pistol and letter opener in hand, Keller took his place behind the station door, hiding behind a rack of coats standing there, dusty, who knew for how long. He was well hidden, and he was pleased by it. There was nothing for him to do but wait, and Keller was very patient.

ELEVEN

T he snow continued to fall. Everything was white, especially the sky above. And the sun, though out, couldn't be seen. Sheriff Brown stood next to his snowplow in his driveway, staring upward and praying that the weather would soon take a turn for the better.

He climbed inside the cab of his truck and lowered the plow. Rose stood inside at the large picture window, smiling and waving at him. She blew him a kiss, and he reciprocated happily. She was so beautiful, his Rose. It always made his heart ache to leave her in the morning, and the only thing that kept him going throughout the day was knowing that she was home, waiting for him, baking a pie, and keeping his supper warm. After all these years, he was still madly in love with his wife.

Bob pulled out of the driveway and took a right,

plowing the piles of snow on the streets as he went. With this sizing task at hand, it would take a bit of extra time to get to the station today. He knew Darren was likely exhausted, but there was always that cot tucked along the wall in the hallway. He could take a quick nap or even get a couple of good hours' sleep if he had to. A man had to sleep, after all.

Bob had a strange feeling. Why? The storm would soon be over. He and everyone he loved was safe. But, yes, it was there in the pit of his stomach. It wasn't nausea, more like nervousness or dread. He sure hoped everything was okay at the station. Before leaving, he tried to call Darren, but the lines were still down. He would have to wait just a little longer to find out what was going on when he got there.

For the next half-hour, Bob plowed the main strip through town on his way to the station. But the snow started laying again just as fast as he cleared it. Bob would wait for it to slow down before investing long hours plowing. The first thing on his mind was getting rid of Derringer. He'd make sure he caught the train at Donneley's Pass. Bob tried calling to purchase the ticket, but the lines were down. Overall, the sheriff felt good, but he would feel even better once he got rid of Mr. Derringer.

He was just about fifty yards away when he noticed how off things looked at the station. Darren's vehicle was gone, and Avery's snowmobile was practically buried in the snow but still running. He could see the exhaust blowing through holes in the snow. How long had she been there? Where was Darren's truck? The bad vibes were hitting the sheriff fast. Without seeing the evidence, he knew that all hell had broken loose at the Sheriff's Office. He was terrified to go inside in fear of what he may find.

Bob pulled up to the station, immense concern on his face as he looked the building over. Everything appeared to be quiet, except for the idling sound from the snowmobile. No one came to the window to see who was pulling up, which was concerning to him. His stomach turned; something was wrong, very wrong. If so, it was he who did most of it. He made a terrible judgment call. Somewhere along the line, he let his heart do the thinking for him. He had been fooled, and he knew it before he even got out of the truck.

He left the truck running, jumped out of the cab, and headed for the station. He jiggled the knob, but it was tightly locked. Bob gave the door a couple of hard thumps, then shouted out for Darren or Avery. He was met with silence in return. He knit his brow and fished his keys out of his pocket, hands trembling. He had a horrible feeling, and there was an unusual order wafting from under the door.

"Darren, open the door, would you?" he shouted as he slipped the key into the hole. "It's colder than an icebox out here! Avery? Darren?"

Bob turned the key, and the lock slid into the open position. He twisted the knob and slowly opened the door. He noticed that the lights were set just above the dim position. But, by now, the lights should've been put on high. Stepping inside, Bob closed the door and reached for the switch. He turned the lights all the way up to get a good look around.

When he caught the faint smell of spilled semen, his anger and sorrow were matched by hatred. His eyes fell immediately on Avery. She was on her back on top of Darren's desk, naked from the waist down, and her legs splayed open grotesquely. There was blood from between them and all down the side of the desk. Bob put his hand on his chest and the other on the desk to steady himself. He started to gasp until he caught his breath, the dread and anxiety overwhelming. Blaming himself for her death, Bob wiped his mouth and made his way to her. He would check for a pulse, but he could tell she was dead when his fingers touched her cold flesh.

"Darren! Where are you?" He hollered.

Bob looked at the cell to find that the door was wide open. Derringer was not inside, nor was he anywhere in the main office. Drawing his gun, Bob began to slowly walk toward the hall, holding his breath to keep from dry heaving. He purposefully averted his eyes away from the once-beautiful woman now massacred on top of Darren's desk. Bob took a left down the hall, but nothing was in immediate view. He bravely began to open every door. It wasn't until he opened the small mop closet in the back that he found the body of his deputy, a massive hole blown through his chest. His eyes were still open.

Bob was overcome with pressure in his left arm. Whatever had taken place here, whoever that stranger was—made the Sheriff lightheaded. He knew with great certainty that he was neither equipped nor experienced enough to deal with the likes of this guy.

Bob began to back out of the closet and up the hall. His hand was still covering his chest in an attempt to steady the pounding. He was in shock, and though his gun was in his hand, he was no longer aware of its presence. It shook loosely in his grip like a doll getting ready to fall from the hands of a crying little girl.

At the end of the hallway, he bumped hard into the wall by the entryway to the office. It helped bring him back to reality. In all his life, nothing like this has ever happened to the quaint town of Thompson Trails. This was the horror only conceived in books and movies. Bob's shortness of breath was relentless. It was beginning to overpower him.

He had to think. He had to contact someone, do something! But the phones were out, and so was the internet, and he was in a world of trouble. It was all he could do to hope that the guy had stolen Darren's truck and got out of Dodge.

He had to find a way to help Thompson Trails before anything worse happened here. Holstering his weapon, he was sure that Derringer had taken Darren's truck, and there was no telling where he took off to or who he'd harm next. How had someone with such a clean record been able to do something so vile, so heinous?

Bob was beside himself while he stood there, nearly lifeless in the hallway, the fear of losing control coursed through his mind. He turned toward a sound as he stepped through the threshold and stopped dead in his tracks. There stood Derringer, a gaping, bloody wound running down his arm and a smile on his face. His soulless eyes were smiling too, and he looked to Bob like a troubled man who waited a very long time for an opportunity like this.

"Well, hello, Sheriff Brown," he said with a broad grin. "I'm sure you're surprised at all the gifts I've left for you. I did all of this out of thanks, you know. For your small-town hospitality and all of that." He paused and glanced at Avery. "She was special, and so was the child she was carrying. I left her in return for the cold, crusty donut. Thanks a lot, you pig."

Bob yearned for the safety of his gun. The maniac was completely mad and looked at him with evil and anger in his eyes. He shook the pistol he was holding at Bob and sneered.

"The first thing you're going to do is remove your utility belt, put it on the floor, and kick it over here to me, now!"

Keeping his eyes on the psychopath, Bob did as he

was told. He felt anger blend in with the sickness in his belly. "What is wrong with you?"

The murderer laughed loudly, throwing his head back as he did. A shiver of sheer terror ran down Bob's spine. He had a terrible feeling he wasn't going to be walking out of the Sheriff's Office alive today.

"What's wrong with me, you ask?" The man began to pace and, as he did, Bob noticed that he was holding his silver letter opener in the other hand. He waved his hands around as he walked and thought about what his answer was going to be. "First, we should probably get on a first-name basis. I'll call you 'Bob,' just Bob. I think that's a fitting name for you, you fat tub of lard."

"Now, back to the first name thing," the man said as he picked up Bob's gun and tucked it into the waistband of his scrub pants. "As you may or may not know by now, I am not 'Elias Derringer.' My name is Elliot Keller; pleased to make your acquaintance."

Bob's stomach sank to the floor and dropped like a lead weight into the soles of his feet. This man was a mass murderer, one of the sickest sociopaths in existence. But he was in prison, serving time for all his crimes, wasn't he? Apparently not anymore.

"None of this would've happened if your deputy hadn't received a call last night from The State Patrol." Keller leaned on Darren's desk and clucked his tongue. "They told him I'd escaped and to be on the lookout. Deputy Rush knew he had me, and he tried to call you.

But lucky for me, the phones went down shortly after he took that call. Poor Darren. I didn't have any other choice, not that it bothered me to put a big pit in his chest. He was such a Barney Fife. How could you even consider having a sidekick like that? Look at the results of his stupidity!"

"What about poor Avery?" Bob asked. "Why Avery?"

"Why Avery?" Keller's voice was mocking and nasty. He was enjoying every minute of this crusade. "Cuz I needed some lovin', that's why. It's really nothing more than that. She had some pretty good cooze for a nearly dead chick. I have to admit, though, the best part was knowing that the baby inside of her was slowly dying. My youngest victim yet."

Bob gagged, and saliva and bile shot out of his mouth. As he puked, Keller laughed. When the Sheriff was finished, Bob looked up at the convict. He was mad at himself for dropping his gun to the floor, and now he was as weak and defenseless as the rest of them were against this butcher. "My turn, huh? The least you could do is give me a head start." Bob begged.

Keller nodded. "Yes, it's your turn, but there will be no head starts."

With that, Keller fired three consecutive shots at Sheriff Brown. The first two hit him in the chest, making him dance like a drunk marionette. The third took out part of his skull and brain, and he dropped to the floor with a heavy thud.

He walked over to the sheriff and dug through his pockets until he had his wallet, badge, and a large ring of keys. Next, he went to the front window and took note of the pickup truck. The sheriff came equipped with a snowplow and all. It was perfect, still running and warm, time to get out of here. With word that he was locked up in this little jail, it wouldn't be long before more law enforcement would come to try and take him back to prison. But, before he left Thompson Trails for good, he intended to have a bit more fun.

Keller hadn't forgotten about sweet Donna Welk or her vile husband. The fun he could have with them would compare significantly to his upbringing, but they wouldn't survive it as he had. He shouldn't have, wished he hadn't, but Keller had, and now there was a penalty to pay for everyone he met.

Keller searched the coat rack to find warm clothing, finally a parka, making sure there were gloves in the pockets. Not only did he find gloves, but he also found a nice warm hunting hat as well. He was in a real hurry, so he put the coat on, mindless of the layer of dust it was covered in. Keller put on the hat and gloves then loaded his pockets with the victims' wallets. Time to get out of here and on to his next big thrill.

He stepped out into the frosty day and locked the jail behind him. Putting his face toward the sun, Keller took a deep breath of fresh air and smiled. When he opened his eyes, a snowmobile was passing. Speak of the devil! It was the blonde woman, Donna, from the cabin resort. Yummy, he thought to himself, just the person he intended to grace with his presence. Things couldn't be more perfect. He stood still, smiled at her, and waved. Man, oh man, was luck on his side the last couple of days, or what?

Donna Welk waved back and pulled the snowmobile over to the side of the road. She left the vehicle running, then climbed off and trudged her way to Keller through the drifts, still smiling pleasantly. It was going to be much easier than he thought. He grinned back in a friendly manner, then reached out and opened the passenger side door of the running pickup.

"I see you're still here in our little burg," she said with a sniffle. "Going somewhere with Sheriff Brown? Did he manage to help you out?"

Keller nodded and tossed the thermal gloves he had been wearing on the passenger seat. "Yeah, he's running me to Donneley's Pass to catch the train to Rocky Mount. Sure is a friendly guy. He let me sleep here, fed me, and even bought my train ticket for me; he wouldn't even hear of me paying him back. Couldn't ask for a better sheriff."

Donna nodded. "We like him. So, you're from Rocky Mount, or are you just visiting family there?"

"Just visiting."

Keller paused in the door and pretended to fiddle around with something on the front seat, just out of

Donna's sight. She was looking skyward, squinting at the white that surrounded them. She looked back at him and shivered.

"Yes, he'd do just about any–" Suddenly, she stopped.

Keller looked back at her to see that her smile was gone. She was staring at the front of the shirt he was wearing. He knew exactly what she was looking at, but he looked down as well, just for good measure.

"What happened to you? Is that blood? Mr. Derringer, are you okay?"

Donna no sooner got the words out of her mouth when Keller grabbed a huge flashlight that was sitting in the middle of the bench-style seat in the truck. He gave a glance up and down the street and turned back to her. He was keeping the flashlight out of sight just behind the door.

"Yeah, I guess it is," he replied with a chuckle. "It's pretty much a bloody mess in there too. You ought to see what I did to those people." Keller nodded toward the station house and laughed cheerfully. Then he looked back at Donna, smile gone, and said, "But not as much of a mess as it's going to be for you in a minute."

Stunned, eyes wide and frozen with shock, "Wha-?" It was the only sound Donna made.

With a single hard swing, Keller brought the flashlight up into the air, then brought it down on her head so hard that blood sprayed out of the gash it created. Donna crumpled to the ground with nothing more than a squeak. As she lay there in the snow, blood seeped from her head, turning white to red.

Keller tossed the light back into the truck and looked up and down the street one more time. Not a person in sight, no sound coming from any direction. He picked her up from the ground as if she weighed no more than a bag of feathers. Keller put her in the passenger side of the pickup, laying her over toward the middle. Locking the passenger door, he pulled the parka hood up, went around the plow in the front, and climbed into the driver's side. Soon, he was pulling away from the station, leaving nothing but murder and blood behind them.

Elliot Keller wasn't sure where he was going, but he figured he had plenty of time to figure it out in a town as dead as Thompson Trails was at that moment in time. The best thing he could think to do was take the truck down the main road, where he had wrecked. He could pull down by the icy water and sit there and think about his next move. Even if she woke while they were there, she didn't stand a chance to escape. They would be in the middle of nowhere.

TWELVE

K eller found it easier to maneuver the roads of Thompson Trails with Sheriff Bob's pickup and the attached plow. The snow was still falling in what could be called torrents. He had the plow down, and the snow moved out of his way like countless scared rabbits running from a great big wolf. It was calming, and the serenity of the control motivated him to turn on the radio. An old country song pumped through the tiny speakers, but Keller fixed that by tracking down a station playing a slamming song by a heavy metal group. It turned his great mood into an excellent one.

As he drove, he thought about the bleeding Donna Welk passed out next to him in the passenger seat. He could hear rattled breathing coming from her lungs, and the blood on her head was clotting quite nicely. Keller felt no amount of remorse or pity for the blonde woman, even though she'd been kind and trusting toward him. Instead, he could smell the womanhood coming off of her in great waves, and his mind was wrapped around what he would do to her when he had the chance. Keller wouldn't be pursuing these actions while they were parked near the river. No, he would wait until he could take her to that prick of a husband of hers. That's when Keller would have the most fun. That was when he would put her through every level of purgatory he could fathom. He would do it before the eyes of the man who'd promised to care for her. Her husband. Who vowed to protect her every day for the rest of her life. The thought of his next performance thrilled him to the bone. Keller would thrive on the memory of her pain for the remainder of his days. Oh, yes, Keller would make sure that he had more fun with Donna Welk than he had with any of his past 'lovers' he had taken before her, even if she was the last he ever got his hands on.

Unexpectedly, she began to stir. At first, she produced slight moans and whimpers. Then she started to move, squirming and jerking here and there as if she were trying to come back to life. He glanced over at her and laughed, then reached out and turned down the radio. Shifting his eyes between the road and Donna, he kept an amused smile on his face and waited for the woman to come around enough to have some sort of conversation.

"Wha -? What's going on?"

Keller snickered, pleased by the sound of her confused and frightened tone. "Well, hello, Mrs. Welk! It's about time you decided to join the fun! I was wondering if you were going to cop out on me or continue to be the life of the party. The sweet little blondie that I first laid eyes on. I knew I could count on you. You know, Donna, I can smell you from here, and you smell as sweet as a schoolgirl if you know what I mean."

Donna lifted herself on one elbow, groaned, and grabbed her head with one hand. "It hurts," she muttered. "What's happening... where am I?"

Now, Keller laughed in earnest. "Where are you? Don't you know? Do you mean to tell me that you don't remember me? Don't you remember our little meeting a day ago? The way your lousy husband called the cops on me when all I was trying to do was keep warm?"

Now she lifted herself a bit more, grabbing the door handle with her hand for support. Shifting in her seat, she touched her head. This time Donna looked at the tacky drying blood smeared over the palm of her hand. She turned to him, and even though her eyes were distant and dizzy, she seemed to be putting the pieces together.

"Mr. Derringer?" she asked, unsure.

Keller snickered. "Yeah, I guess so. At least, as far as you know. But you might know me better as Elliot Keller. Do you know me, Donna Welk?"

She observed him for a moment, and much to his

surprise, the woman remained calm. "Yes, I know about you, Mr. Keller."

Keller glanced at her, his smile fading a tad. Why was she so calm? "You know about me, do you? What do you know about me, Donna Welk?"

She clenched her eyes shut against the pain of her pounding head. "I know you. I know what you do, and I know who you are."

"Tell me."

Donna leaned her aching head against the cold glass of the passenger side window. "You like to hurt women. You would like to hurt me."

"Let me tell you something, Donna Welk," he muttered with an entertained grin. "You don't know what being hurt is all about. Everything you know about me you've heard on television or read in the papers. I want you to know that they only share half the story, the tame parts. Honey, I'm going to do things to you that you never imagined possible."

Keller took his eyes off the road long enough to study her. She appeared utterly fearless as if she had resigned herself to what he had planned in the short minutes since she gained consciousness. He was impressed. She wasn't even looking toward the door for a way out. Most would've jumped to get away from him. I guess she realized it wasn't going to help. She wouldn't be going anywhere without him.

"Yes, I would like to hurt you," he replied. "But more

than that, I am going to ruin you as soon as the time is right. I'm going to demonstrate what pain is, so you don't have to imagine. But none of that is going to happen without Mr. Rick, your darling husband. He needs to witness all of it."

They were well past the place where Keller wrecked Rush's truck. Up ahead, he could see that there was a turn-off that led down to a small parking area by the river. The road they were on was flanked by the river on both sides, with multiple small drive-downs that allowed tourists or other visitors to park. The one up ahead was perfect, so it seemed. It not only took them off the road, out of view of passing cars, but it also gave them some privacy to park under a large tree. Keller slowed the truck down and put on the blinker, even though there wasn't another car in sight to see through his devious intentions.

Dizzy or not, Donna knew of his plans. "Whatever you do, be careful going down there. The water toward the river's edge is going to give way if you're not careful. We'll both go under and drown, and you won't have much fun with me then, will you, Mr. Keller?"

Donna's condescending attitude pissed him off. But at the same time, she gained some of his respect. She wasn't showing any obvious signs of fear, and in a way, that scared him. All of his victims buckled and begged. They cried for their lives and the lives of their friends and loved ones. But not Donna Welk. If anything, the only thing she conveyed was mild disgust, and it unnerved him a bit. If he had met her in another life, he just might have fallen in love with her.

"I think I can handle it without any help from you, Donna."

She snorted at him. "I've lived here longer than you've been around. And don't call me Donna."

Keller swung out with his right arm and smashed her in the face, causing blood to spurt full force from her nose. She quietly cried out and put the sleeve of her parka to her face. Then she started to laugh at him. You're a weakling to hit a woman. What a coward!

"If you're going to kill me anyway, what do I care what your opinion is?" She laughed some more, then wiped at her nose, blood smearing across her cheek. "By the time you're done with me, this little bit of blood will be nothing." She turned to him and sneered. "You're nothing but a lowlife, and you can't threaten me enough to scare me. You're too pathetic. Let's just get on with business."

Keller didn't answer, but he was furious with her blasé mindset. He took a slow right down into the turn-off and pulled up under the tree, aiming the nose of the heavy truck at the edge of the river. It was hard to tell how close Keller was to the water because the snow was so deep and drifting, but he didn't care. Surely the ice was thick enough to hold them. Besides, he didn't give much credence to anything his victims said to him. They were blabbering in futile efforts to save their lives.

"So," he said sarcastically as he slowly steered the pickup plow down into the pull-off. "I can't threaten you enough to scare you, huh? You seem sure of yourself, and I find that amusing. You have no idea what I'm capable of, so keep that in mind."

"You have no idea what I know or don't know, so you keep that in mind, you coward," Donna spat.

Donna knew exactly what this monster was capable of, and she knew one thing and one thing only. She had never known a pain like she felt losing a child or the hope of having one. It made her want to die. He could do what he wanted to do. Death would take her directly to the child she never held. She wasn't worried about herself, but she was concerned about Rick.

"Keller, you're pulling too close to the water's edge," she said wearily. "I'm trying to tell you –"

"Shut up! The water's so frozen that it would probably hold us safely until spring, you dumb cooze." Keller insisted.

Donna rolled her eyes and shrugged, then put her fingers back to the wound on her head. It was terribly sore, but it seemed the blood had clotted, and surprisingly enough, she was thinking incredibly clear despite the blow he dealt her. She kept her mouth shut as Keller crept closer and closer to the snowdrift, which hid the ice at the water's edge.

"I'm telling you."

Suddenly, there was a loud crack. It sounded more

like a very loud gunshot, and as soon as it occurred, the front end of the truck, heavy from the extra weight of the plow attachment, sank about a half-foot with a violent jerk. Keller's eyes flew open in surprise, and Donna rolled her own once again.

"I told you, you stupid idiot."

"Shut up!" Keller hit her, causing nothing more than a groan, and the truck's front end jerked again, sinking a bit more. He paused and listened, trying to determine just how much more they were going to drop. Sure enough, another pop, then a large crevice began to form and creep across the river at an alarming rate of speed. Keller forcefully grabbed her by the shoulder of her parka and jerked her across the bench seat, opening the driver's door simultaneously. "We have to get out of here, and now!"

For the first time, Donna didn't disagree with him. Slight vertigo aside, she allowed him to pull her, and she scrambled to follow him. Neither of them had any idea how far out he drove them into the river, but she knew that it was far enough that the heavy truck was going to sink, at least the front end. They couldn't stay in the truck and expect to survive.

The truck jerked downward once again, this time sinking another foot-and-a-half. Donna saw the panic wash over Keller's face as they both fell from the driver's side. Together, they landed hard in the snowdrift running alongside the truck. He may be a killer, but he did not have killer instincts. He was as dumb as a box of rocks deep inside that manic mind, she thought. She hoped she could eventually outsmart him. As they sat in the freezing snow, both breathing hard, they watched the entire front end of the truck submerge, and it didn't take long for the rest of the vehicle to follow suit. The truck sank to the bottom of the river in no time. It was out of sight, nothing but broken ice and bubbles rising to the surface.

The pair sat in silence, staring at the empty spot that now only consisted of tire tracks and plow skid marks. Donna wanted to laugh out loud, but it wouldn't be worth pissing off the surprised predator any more than he already was. She couldn't help it and let out a little giggle. She stopped before they became uncontrollable and waited patiently for him to tell her what to do next. It didn't take long to find out.

Keller grabbed her once again by the parka and jerked her to her feet, joining her as they went. "Looks like we're running out of obvious options, but I'm not done with you yet. How far are we from your cabins?"

She ignored the question. "What do you want me to do?" she asked. "Lay down naked right here and let you do your vile thing?" Keller sneered while she considered her options.

"Do you know these woods?"

"Well, I've lived here just a couple of years, but I know them well enough. Why?"

He grabbed her again and began to drag her along. "You're going to take us to your cabins. You're going to lead the way."

"How do you know I won't trick you?" she asked.

Keller smiled and shook his head, then pointed his gun at her and cocked it. "Because I'll blow your head off and leave your brainless corpse right here in the snow, that's why."

Donna shook her head, shrugged, and replied, "Then let's hit the road. You're a special kind of dumb, aren't you?"

Not amused, he gave her another hard smack to the head, and the two of them began the long, snowbound journey back to Virginia Trailhead Cabins and her sure demise.

But Donna Welk was past the point of caring. She had gone numb inside, and it surprised her how fast.

THIRTEEN

W ith hindsight, the busy couple should have provisioned for the storm. Rick had been waiting for his wife to return with a simple bag of groceries, but it seemed like hours had passed. She left by snowmobile to purchase eggs, a loaf of bread, a gallon of milk, and a container of coffee. Luckily, the grocery store owners live in an apartment above the store.

Rick did some plowing of the resort parking lot, then settled into the office on one of the lobby couches and began to read an old magazine. He hated the rag, but he read everything else in the place, and it didn't look like the mail was going to come with new periodicals for a day or two.

He knew that the roads were terrible, but one thing he could say about Donna. She could handle a snowmobile like a true professional. Even for such a small woman, he'd put money on her any day in a competition. The thought of her maneuvering that thing around like it was nothing brought a smile to his face. She was fine, and she'd be back before he knew it. In the meantime, he'd find something to fix; maybe he'd even take a little nap on the lobby couch.

So, he settled in with the tabloid magazine and read the senseless thing from cover to cover, even getting into a couple of articles about a celebrity who seemed to be nothing but a lowlife cheat. But who was he to say? Regardless of what the man was like in real life, the magazine made him out to be nothing but a brute. He also read about a girl who lost her leg to a shark while surfing. Poor thing just had her first child, and that story interested Rick more than the rest of the gossipy articles. It amazed him how people could go through the worst of experiences and come out stronger than ever. The human spirit was a powerful thing.

By the time he tossed the magazine on the coffee table in front of the lobby couch, he was exhausted. A nap seemed like a great idea. He started to doze and fell into a light, dreamy sleep.

Something made him jerk awake. What time was it? And how long had he been asleep? Glancing at the clock, his nerves were suddenly tapped. Donna had been gone for more than two hours! What could she be doing? Donna was one of the most responsible women he had ever known, next to his mother, and now he was worried that something had happened to her. Had she crashed on the snowmobile? Had she gotten herself stuck in a deep snowdrift? There were indeed plenty of them around, and they were getting deeper by the minute.

Rick wasn't sure if he should wait a little longer for her or take off on his snowmobile and try to track her down. He was too nervous to sit around. Rick quickly bundled up, locked the office up, and headed for the snow machine to track down his wife, but not before leaving her a note. He checked the fuel and fired up the engine with a roar. Waving off the exhaust fumes and barely waiting for it to warm, he was on his way.

The Virginia Trails Cabins were a mere mile from the center of town, and the grocers were a couple of blocks past that. He would get on the main highway, ride along the side of the snow-covered road, and head in the general direction of town. Either he would pass her, or he would find her walking. The very thought of seeing her hurt, or worse, made him sick to his stomach. He should never have listened to her when she insisted on going to town alone. Rick should've gone with her or gone himself. But she was always able to handle stuff like this before! He felt terrible for taking a nap, knowing she may be hurt or maybe the snowmobile broke down, and she was out there walking in the elements. How was he to know?

Rick didn't see a soul on the route between the

cabins and town. Not so much as a truck, a plow, or even another snowmobile. All was as still and dead as a ghost town. Rick forged ahead, trying not to worry. Soon the sheriff's station was in sight. Immediately, his heart began to pound with relief.

He instantly noticed Donna's snowmobile on the side of the road. There were no other vehicles. Not even Bob's plow truck was anywhere in sight. He pulled over to the side of the road, just behind Donna's snowmobile, and walked towards the ski. It was off and cold. He opened the gas cap and peered inside; it was empty. She must have run out of gas, he thought to himself. He made his way towards the station. Parked just outside the door was another snowmobile, partially covered in snow. It was apparent it had been there for a while. He went to the door with a whole lot of questions. It was securely locked, so he peeked through the window. The scene he saw inside took his breath away.

Donna was definitely in serious trouble. He knew exactly who was responsible. This had everything to do with that stranger, Elias Derringer. He looked through the window again to make sure neither of the bodies inside was Donna. He could see Bob and a woman who looked like Avery. But he had no way of knowing who else was in there rotting.

Looking up and down the main road for tire tracks, he could barely make out signs of them. The snow managed to take care of all that. He jumped back on his snowmobile and drove the two blocks to the grocery store. The place was dead, and all the interior lights were out, no tracks, no footprints. The town was completely shut down.

Finally, he pulled his cell out from his coat and tried to dial up the State Patrol. There was no signal whatsoever, and he screamed to himself in fear and frustration. What was he going to do? The answer came to him. He would go back to the cabins, get on the internet, and contact the State Patrol from there. He jumped back on the snowmobile and sped back toward the cottages as fast as the vehicle would carry him.

He had to find his wife before she ended up like the people, his friends, who were brutally murdered at the sheriff's station.

"So, Mr. Keller. What exactly is the plan, anyway?" Donna was past the point of fear. This guy was a madman, and he was going to do whatever he wanted with no regard to her life or the people who would miss her. She figured she might as well stand up to him while she could.

He was silent for a second, thinking about his response. They were both freezing and breathing heavily, and he couldn't wait to get back to the cabins. Donna wasn't any help, but could he expect her to be? After all, she was aware of what he could do.

"Well," he began. "At first, I was going to tie up that prick of a husband of yours and show him what it's like to watch the one he loves suffer immensely. Now, however, those thoughts are beginning to bore me. I want to get back to the cabins, and I want you to get me to Donneley's Pass to pick up my train ticket to Rocky Mount. You help me do this, and I'll spare the both of you. I'll even forget that you exist. But if you don't, well, you can both count on a world of pain."

Donna didn't hesitate. "That plan gets my vote. But the problem is that you're a murdering prick. How can you be trusted? Well, you can't. Do you really think I believe you're going to let me live?"

He backhanded her hard and sent her flying to the ground. Her cry came out a bit more than a sob, a pitiful whimper that was swallowed up in the wind.

"So, how far are we from the cabins, do you think?" he asked in a calm tone of voice, almost as if he hadn't just hit her.

The impact of his hand on her frigid, cold face stung horribly. Now she lay face down in the snow, icing the sting. She was livid, biting her tongue from lashing out verbally. Wiping the snow from her face, Donna took a deep breath and looked around. She ignored the blow and struggled to stand up again. She stood and dusted herself off. "Not far; maybe two miles, but I think less.

Just through these woods, around the rocky bend, across the stream, and over the hill. The cabins are just on the other side. I should tell you, the downslope of the hill is tricky, so we're going to have to take it slow, or we could bury ourselves." She instantly regretted telling him this information. Perhaps she could have pushed him.

"Good! We'll take it easy then." He stopped and looked at her, and physically turned her to meet his gaze. "How are you gonna get me there? To the train, I mean."

Donna looked at him as if he were mentally disabled. "Rick has another snowmobile. I'm sure he'd be glad to take you to the train just to get you out of our lives. He'll probably give you the snowmobile."

"He's not gonna take me, lady," Keller snarled. "You are! Get it straight. You do this right, I'm telling you, I won't hurt you, and you'll be home by nightfall. Got it?"

"Got it." She knew better. This guy wasn't going to let her drop him off for a train and leave her alive. He wouldn't risk her calling the cops right away, which is precisely what she would do. She knew it, and so did he. But she could play his silly games for the time being.

The two continued to trudge along, high stepping through the drifts and making their way to the cabins in silence. Now they understood each other, and there was no reason to waste energy on words.

FOURTEEN

I t took Rick less time to make it back to the cabin resort than it did for him to get to town. His distress was the motivating factor, and he worried that he wouldn't get help in time. Rick was also concerned that his adrenaline would cause him to crash the snowmobile. He was getting the shakes, and all he could think about was getting back and trying to get online to the Virginia State Patrol.

Haphazardly, he parked the snowmobile as close to the front door as possible, leaving it askew. He ran inside to boot up the computer as fast as he possibly could. Pulling the cell from his pocket, he tried for a signal once more. No bars. He snatched up the desk phone headset and checked for a dial tone—nothing. His only hope was the cable internet. As he sat, waiting for the computer to boot up, he fidgeted, paced, and swore, trickles of sweat running down his face while his mind imagined the worst possible case scenarios. What if he was torturing his beautiful wife as he sat there? Or, what if she was already dead? What if the man had already had his way with her? And she was left, frozen solid, in a snowbank along the river?

But then, a miracle. Rick heard the familiar series of singsong tones that let him know he was online. The computer had been off. And now here it was, up and running and waiting for him to tell it what to do. He rushed over to the keyboard and fumbled for the mouse. Then he typed in the website for the State Patrol with rapid fury. They were the only ones he could think of to contact. After all, the bodies of the sheriff and the deputy's wife were sprawled, grotesque and dead, down at the station. As for the deputy, who knew. There was no one else to contact.

The computer was moving very slow. And more than once, Rick was convinced it was going to kick him offline for good. At last, the site to the State Patrol appeared, and he searched feverishly for a way to send a message, but all he could find was a 'contact us' option. Rick used it, writing as detailed a message as possible with the number of characters allowed. When he was finished, he pushed send, then searched for a way to call nine-one-one online. Rick knew it could be done using an app. But for the life of him, he couldn't seem to find any of the information he was looking for.

Then he found a link that explained everything. Clicking on it, he breathed a sigh of relief, sat back, and waited for the slow, practically nonexistent connection to complete its course. It was at that very moment that he could hear everything powering down. Everything went black except for the sky outside, still hauntingly white.

Rick pounded his fist against the desk, jumped up, and began to pace frantically. He was so distraught that he couldn't logically think of what to do. Finally, Rick did the only thing he knew to do, donning his jacket and leaving the office. He left the door unlocked in case Donna returned. Rick would go to any and every door he could until he found help. He would ride that snowmobile all the way to the next county if he had to, but Rick was going to find his wife. If that slimeball was still with her, he was going to tear him limb from limb.

Rick started the snowmobile for the second time that day and sped out of the snow-covered lot. His mind and heart both racing from the terror of the unknown.

Donna Welk walked silently, high stepping through the drifts as they came to the top of the hill before getting to the cabins. Keller had a death grip on her arm, and he was pointing the gun at her back with his other hand. He hadn't said a word in a while, but as soon as the cabins came into view, she braced herself for him to start running his mouth.

"Good girl, Donna," he said, and she could hear the smile he was wearing on his face in the tone of his voice. "You know, you keep being so helpful, you might just live through all of this, but on second thought, I doubt it."

"What do you mean?" she asked. She convinced herself that Keller would let her live if she drove him to Donneley's Pass. "You said –"

"I know what I said," Keller replied. "But it wouldn't do to have you take me to the train, then turn around and notify the cops. I can get to the Pass myself, without your help, you know. Having a little fun with you and that husband of yours is starting to sound like the most intelligent and logical thing to do, considering it might be my last chance to have a little party."

Her heart sank, but she didn't respond. Just as she knew, Keller was full of it. Donna refused to let him know that she was feeling any kind of fear or despair. Donna wanted him to believe that she was in complete control of her emotions, even though she was getting more and more frightened. Donna wasn't going down without a fight. He'd better know it. If she was going to die, Donna was going to take a great big chunk of this jerk with her.

Her next words came out in a torrent. "Have you been a pathological liar your entire life?" she asked. "I suspect someone made you this way. This doesn't just happen for no reason. I never heard of a serial killer who didn't have a messed-up childhood or something. I hate your guts, but I feel bad for whatever you went through." She stopped and looked him in the eye. "I still wish you were dead, though. You're like a horse with a broken leg."

He ignored the comment without lashing out, but his rage was building. All the while, Keller kept checking over his shoulder.

"So, what happened at the jail? Why didn't I see the sheriff or deputy?"

"Oh, that little soiree began a little after midnight last night. I blew Darren's guts all over myself. Trust me. It was epic. And this morning, I had his wife Avery and unborn child for breakfast. She was tight. But I bet not as tight as you! Don't worry. She put up a fight." He stopped dead in his tracks, yanking Donna backward a step. As he let go of her arm, she instantly started rubbing the area where he had his tight grip. She could feel the blood coursing back into her forearm and hand, like a tourniquet was just removed. He opened his parka to show off his wound. "She got me right here with a letter opener. I put the old Sheriff down. He was old and tired. That was all very entertaining, why do you ask?

"I just wanted some closure, is all." She said as she turned and began walking. She quietly thought to herself. This guy is sick, a mentally deranged fucken lunatic.

He grabbed her arm in the same spot forcing her

forward. "You miss that party but trust me, tonight's celebration will be all yours. You're the star of my show. I plan on gracing you with my presence all night long."

Donna continued to walk as she kept quiet, just thinking about the vile animal behind her. She was profiling him in her mind. Yes, he was hot-headed, that's for sure. Obviously, he did these acts without thinking about how others will be affected. Recalling when she first met him in the cabin, he tried to be polite with his superficial charm, but he came off like a sleazeball. Clearly, he doesn't understand normal human feelings, not based on his cheesy flirts. No conscience whatsoever. What is he? A narcissistic sociopath? Showing off his fresh wound like he just did. She wanted to confront him, calling him out— you're just a cold and callous sociopathic narcissist seeking my approval. But she continued to bite her tongue.

His show, his party? What's that all about? He sure does have some kind of grandiose sense of self-worth, doesn't he? Donna could hear him breathing. At least the piece of shit was quiet. She was sure he was carefully plotting his next move. What does he want? What is his main objective? To kill her or to rape her, and in what order? She needed a weapon and fast.

She continued mentally talking to herself, concluding that he was just a cold-hearted and calculating psychopath...no remorse, no empathy. She hadn't seen any sign of intelligence, but he must have some smarts to escape from a maximum-security prison. But what about his poor judgment with the ice? He's probably ignorant and fails to learn from experience. Only time will tell. She wondered how she could possibly get the upper hand.

Donna continued to rack her brain for ideas. Maybe she could get a rock and bash his head in. But with the gun on her back, it wouldn't be easy. Perhaps she could pee and distract him long enough to find a rock or to run. But that idea also fell apart, thinking about being defenseless with her pants around her ankles.

If she could walk him close to a cliff and push him... but he had a gorilla grip on her arm.

Donna continued to run scenarios through her mind over and over as they trudged through the snow. The cold was setting into her feet. Her toes began to sting. She was gradually marching on her way to her horrifying demise.

FIFTEEN

A s they neared the cabins ever so slowly, Keller walked, oblivious to the fact that the roads were still devoid of traffic and piled high with snow. Not only was it still falling from the sky, but the high winds were creating drifts as high as small houses. All Keller could do was take solace in the circumstances. It meant a day, two at the very most, to have his way with Donna and Rick Welk. It would be similar to his time at the cabin in the woods with those four kids, only better. In this case, the weather would keep them isolated long enough for him to have all kinds of fun and games. He glanced at the back of Donna's head and thought about how it would feel to pull her hair out in great chunks, tearing her scalp off with it. It gave him a partial erection just thinking about it.

They reached the crest of the hill, then slowly made

their way down the steep side, which faced the cabins. Keller tightened his grip on her arm; it wouldn't do to have her tumble head over heels down the hill, only to get up, run, and escape. After all, she knew the area much better than he did.

"I still have this gun on you," he roared over the whining winds, poking her with it just for spite. "Just keep walking and cooperating, and you'll be fine... at least for now."

Oh, how Donna wanted to turn around and cave his face in. She wished to disable him and cut off his member, or better yet, shoot him right between the legs and leave him there in pain to freeze to death. Maybe now would be as good a time as any to take away his power over her. She could turn around and attack him. Fight with all of her might. He would surely put a bullet in her if she tired and end this nightmare. But what about Rick? How she hoped that Rick was there, waiting. But she knew better. Like Keller, she was paying attention to her surroundings as well, and there were a couple of things that didn't look good at all.

For one thing, his snowmobile was nowhere in sight, and from where they were on the hill, she should've seen it clearly, parked in front of the office. He was gone, and that was good; maybe she could stall this bottom-feeder and save her husband's life, if nothing else.

The other thing she noticed was that there wasn't a single light on, anywhere, in any home or building that she could see. This was the most terrifying scenario she could think of on top of everything else. Even the tall neon sign which boasted Virginia Trailhead Cabins was out, and there was no light on in the office, either. There was no power whatsoever in Thompson Trails, and that was very bad indeed.

Keller could also see they were in the middle of a complete power outage. Unlike Donna, Keller found it to be one of the best strokes of luck so far. There would be no calls, no internet, no nothing. Just time to warm up and have the fun he had been fantasizing about for hours, nothing but peaceful screaming and flowing blood. Oh, it would be good.

As they neared the foot of the hill, Keller gave her a hard shove, just for amusement. Donna tripped over her own feet and fell face-first into two feet of snow. She felt her nose hit something hard beneath the snow, and warm blood began to gush from her nose. Keller watched her, smiling, as Donna struggled to her hands and knees. Just as she stabilized herself enough to stand, he planted a firm kick to her stomach. He knocked the wind out of her and sent her into the snow once again. He began to laugh hysterically.

When Keller finally got control of himself, he watched her as she got to her feet. He wouldn't kick her again, even though he was tempted, but there was no more time to waste at this point. He had to control himself so they could get to the cabins safely and unnoticed. There was something that bothered him as she stood. Even with the wind knocked out of her and blood all over her face and hair, she was smiling. There was even blood on her teeth from a busted lip. Her grin unsettled him, and he had to take control back quickly.

"You know, the sight of blood is visually erotic to me," he said sarcastically as he grabbed her arm and pushed her along forcefully once again. "Can't wait to get a little relief; that nosebleed of yours is proving to be nothing but a tease. Your husband is going to love what I do to you, lady." The raw edge to his voice destroyed her anger and replaced it with cold panic. For a moment, she couldn't speak.

Donna shivered but continued to walk, and she didn't give him the satisfaction of a reply or reaction. What would be, would be. She planned to remove as much fun out of his sick games as possible. He would have to entertain himself with their deaths because she wouldn't help make it a more enjoyable experience for him.

DONNA AND KELLER NEARED THE CABINS. "SO, since you like to do nothing but brag about your grotesque sexual prowess, why don't you man up and tell me about all this great stuff you're going to do to me." She smiled at him again, and this time she added a wink.

"You don't know me at all. For all you know, I might just love it."

Donna was seriously beginning to freak him out, and she was moving a bit too fast for his taste. He would make her good and dead, but now it wasn't just about the sex and violence. It was also about how much she was starting to scare him, and he didn't scare easily.

"Slow down," Keller told her, his eyes frantically taking in everything around them. "We're going to come up behind the place, by the picnic benches by the lake. I don't want anyone else to notice either one of us, especially your old man."

Keller didn't realize that Rick's snowmobile was nowhere in sight. He thought her husband was somewhere in the cabins, which was okay with him. At first, Donna thought about leading him around in front of all the security cameras. Rick had strategically placed them around the property when they first purchased the cabins. But it would be pointless now. The power was out, and the cameras were useless. She wished they would have invested in a generator.

She would cooperate with his plan until she could come up with something that might buy her and her husband some time. No matter where he had gone, he would be back soon. She knew that Rick was sick to death about her, and if he had gone to the sheriff's office for any reason, he would be well aware of what kind of trouble she was facing.

"Go to the right," Keller shouted in the wind, jerking her hard in the direction. "We'll come up from behind, and then we'll go around the far end and come around by the office. He's probably in there right now, just waiting for you to come back and make him something to eat, the worthless prick." He paused. "Speaking of which, I'm starving. Make me something when we get there."

Keller hadn't been paying attention. Donna was going for groceries when he snatched her up. Unfortunately, they didn't prepare very well for the storm. There was barely any food in the house. Well, she could make him peanut butter on bread heels because that's all they had. Or she could let him have free rein of the lobby snacks. They might even have a couple of beers in the fridge in their cabin. It didn't matter; she'd be able to buy a little time if he was hungry. Hunger could throw a man off his game, that much she knew.

Obediently and quietly, Donna did as she was told, and the two of them crossed the back area of the cabins, then rounded the corner in front of the office. Donna automatically reached out and grabbed the handle to find it unlocked. She struggled to get the door open against the snow that had drifted up against it.

Before entering the dark office, Keller gave her arm a big yank. "Wait... why is it so dark everywhere? Why doesn't your guy have any lights on? Most of all, why is the door unlocked if he isn't in here?"

Donna smirked and shook her head. Gesturing up at

the dark neon sign, she replied sarcastically, "Obviously, the power is out. I was supposed to be getting groceries, Keller. You're not as smart as you think, are you?"

He slapped her hard with his gloved hand, snapping her head to the side. She closed her eyes and ignored the pain that exploded inside her. Instead, she held a frozen face. Keller continued to look around at the stillness of the cabin area. Remembering he saw the power outage at the top of the hill, the cold and hunger must be getting to him. There was absolutely no one in sight, and he couldn't hear the sound of vehicles, snowmobile or otherwise.

"Rick isn't even here, is he Donna?" he finally asked. "He must be out looking for you. Quick, let's get inside."

The two entered the office, and Donna stopped to lock the door with her set of keys.

"Good thinking, babe; I'm beginning to like you more and more. You might be a keeper." Keller said as he looked around. "We need candles, or lanterns, or something. What do you have?"

Donna dug blindly through the desk's top drawer, feeling her way until she identified a box of match sticks. Walking over to the plate glass window, she turned to Keller. "There's a box of emergency tapers in the bottom drawer of the filing cabinet, along with a flashlight."

Keller listened to her and went to the file cabinet. "Sure wish I had remembered to bring that big flashlight from the pickup. Oh well. This will do." He flipped on the tiny flashlight, found the box of tapers, and took them to Donna. She proceeded to light them, one at a time, then melted the bottom so they'd stick to the counter. It was all she could think of to do.

"There," Keller said with relief. "Much better." He walked over to the small mini-fridge and opened it up; there was nothing inside but room-temperature bottled water. "There's nothing here." He said and picked up a little snack pack of donuts from the table.

Donna noted that his voice was edgy, and she knew that he was getting hangry. "Listen, Mr. Keller. Our cabin is right over there." She pointed out the window to the last cabin, which backed up to the main road. "We have a kitchenette in there, and I'm sure I can scrounge up something, even if it's a can of soup."

The criminal thought about it for a minute and then looked outside. "Okay. But I'm not crossing the lot because I have a feeling Rick's coming back soon. It wouldn't do to have my little daydream with you two ruined because you made a scene in the parking lot. We'll walk around back again, then slip between the two closest cabins and enter yours. Ready? Let's go."

He grabbed her arm, and they reversed their previous route. Soon, they were slipping between cabins eight and nine, and Donna was unlocking the door. They went inside the cabin, and she closed it behind them. Donna saw her reflection in the vanity mirror across the room and realized how badly battered she looked. It was terrifying to see. Donna fished out a heavy-duty flashlight hooked to a massive battery from under the bed. Turning it on, she looked at Keller, who was peeking out the window.

"What's wrong?" she asked, noticing the odd look on his face.

Keller snorted and continued to stare out the slit in the curtains. "We left the candles on over there; did you do that on purpose, you conniving little wench?"

Now she was getting aggravated. "I forgot all about them. What am I supposed to do when you're pushing me around all the time? I mean, a person can't think when you're rattling their brains, Einstein." She turned her attention to the mirror, wiping the dry blood from her face with a tissue and examining her nose.

He gave her a death stare, lost in some incomprehensible void. "I'm going to burn that attitude out of you. Something your husband should've done before he ever hooked up with your lippy mouth."

Donna scanned the room, looking, wishing, hoping she could find a weapon. Something, anything sharp enough to stick in this lunatic's jugular. To her dismay, not even a letter opener could be found. She tossed the tissue in the trash and thought about the kitchen. Plotting for a knife, she touched her split lip and winced in pain. Turning away from the mirror, she asked Keller. "Want some peanut butter?

"Sure, what else you got?"

All she could think about was grabbing a knife to jab in his neck. In the cabinet, she pulled the peanut butter out along with a package of cookies. Strategically she set them in front of Keller in hopes to distract him. With his eyes fixated on the snacks, he shoved the gun in his waistband and ripped the cookie package open. Donna opened the silverware drawer and removed a spoon eyeing her wanted knife. She fiddled with the napkins and left the drawer open, waiting for him to eat a cookie. Her feet were planted, her face was poised. Will this be the moment of her death?

SIXTEEN

E arlier, Rick took off from the Virginia Trails Cabins on his snowmobile. The power was out, and there was no way to call for help to report the massacre at the sheriff's office and his missing wife. He was filled with nothing but ups and downs, fears and mental torments that Rick, until that day, hadn't conceived before. He never thought something of this magnitude could happen around here.

First, he began to go from house to house, starting with the very closest one to the resort. He received answers at every residence, but none had working phones or cellular devices to let him use. As per what he felt to be his duty, Rick filled them in on the atrocities he discovered... the situation with Donna, and the town's desperate need for police assistance. He told them all about the murderer and suggested they refuse to let anyone in who might try to seek refuge with them. He emphasized the seriousness of the situation and told them to prepare for anything. They agreed to call the State Patrol as soon as the power was restored.

Rick approached another house. It was the Martins. He could see a pretty woman in her mid-thirties, crocheting or knitting or something through the window. A man about the same age was stoking the fire. A beautiful young girl of about fifteen played on a phone and munched on chips from a big bowl.

Rick walked up onto the porch and knocked on the door. Jake Martin opened the door, gave him a once over, and smiled. "Rick, how are you?" Jake seemed pleasant enough, at least for now.

Rick just smiled. "Could I have a word with you alone?"

"Ah yes, come in, let me get my coat." Jake looked at his wife, who nodded kindly.

"Would you like some coffee?" she asked Rick.

Rick gestured with his head, signifying yes, "Please, would you have a cup to go perhaps?" It's nice and warm here. He stated as he turned to the teen. Rick smiled at the pretty young girl, who smiled back shyly. Do you have cell service?" Rick asked the girl.

She shook her head, no.

After a minute, Janet Martin returned with an old coffee mug, "Here you go, don't worry about the mug," Janet said, as she touched Rick's frozen hand.

"Well, thank you," he replied.

The door opened behind Rick, and a cold gust filled the air. There stood Jake, all ready to go. "Okay, Rick, let's step outside." Jake Martin closed the door behind them. Rick didn't miss a beat and filled Jake in on the horrific details.

Rick also stopped by the sheriff's office for the second time, hoping that what he'd seen through the window was nothing but a horrifying nightmare. To his dismay, it was all just as he'd left it. His heart was grieved by what was happening in his beloved town of Thompson Trails.

Rick sat down on his snowmobile in the blizzard, which continued to batter the town. He put his head in his hands, feeling like a baby whose mother was nowhere to be found. All he could think about was his sweet Donna, the soft, kind, understanding woman who seemed to trust everyone she met all too much. The woman who had gone through so much grief and pain. She couldn't bear to put another through the same. Oh, Donna, he felt such an overwhelming need to protect and serve every day of his life. Now, he couldn't do anything for her.

He allowed himself a few moments to sit in despair before pulling himself together. Rick Welk took off and quickly made his way to the home of Sheriff Bob Brown and his motherly wife, Rose. Rick had no idea what he would say, but he had to figure it out quickly.

Captain Russell Johnson of the State Patrol was popping antacids like candies, and he was pacing around his office with sweat pooling around his armpits. The police precinct was bustling with people, and the smell of stale coffee filled the air. The background noise was relentless, phones ringing and typewriters clicking away. Chaos seemed to be a daily fret.

Johnson reached for the phone in a snap and picked up the receiver. He tried again to dial the number to the Sheriff's Office, where Elliot Keller was supposedly being held, but to no avail. The lines were still down in Thompson Trails. Slamming the receiver back into the cradle, Johnson popped another antacid into his mouth, and his mind began to wander. He really shouldn't be worrying because he was told the man was securely behind bars. But his gut was in knots over it, and for a good reason.

Since speaking with Deputy Darren Rush in the wee hours of that morning and confirming they had a suspect matching Elliot Keller's description in custody, he hadn't heard a peep. Not even a call to question when they would arrive to pick up the suspect for transfer. Nothing from the deputy, and nothing from the sheriff. In a way, it wasn't a huge surprise. The fact was that the power and phones were down for miles. The county had lost all of its resources shortly after that initial call. But it was unsettling. They wanted that guy back where he belonged before he could hurt someone else.

Johnson's phones and computers were back up and running. But the lack of contact from Sheriff Brown wasn't what had him on the edge of the seat.

The problem plaguing Johnson was simple but horribly burdensome, nonetheless. The central communications division of the State Patrol received a computer-generated nine-one-one from a service that typically went unused.

The attempt originated in Thompson Trails. It was then, according to information provided by the Appalachian Power Company, that the town of Thompson Trails lost all power, just after the nine-one-one attempt.

A bead of sweat formed at Johnson's thinning hairline, then ran down his forehead. Something was very wrong, and there was only one thing he could think to do about it. Johnson's anxiety was about to boil over. He left his office and walked up the hall to the office of a detective named Jack Fowler. He was a simple, down-to-earth detective who mostly worked shoplifting and paper crimes, like forgeries and bad checks. But Detective Fowler was unique in one solitary way: he moonlighted during the evening hours by driving a massive plow truck around the side streets and school routes of the County, as well as the roads around, and leading to, Virginia Max.

The good news was, it was two in the afternoon, and even though the snow was still blanketing everything in that area of Virginia, Fowler had driven his plow to work to save time, just like he did every winter.

Captain Johnson reached Fowler's door and saw him scribbling away at random paperwork. A day like this was always the perfect time to catch up, but right then, Johnson didn't care how far behind Fowler might be. He didn't even knock on the man's door. Turning the knob, he barged right in.

"Sorry to bug you, Fowler," he blurted out. "We have something of a situation in Thompson Trails regarding one escaped Elliot Keller, and I need you, or I need your plow. So, which is it going to be?"

Fowler looked up at the captain with a smile on his face. "Fill me in on the details on the way, and will you bring coffee?"

"Deal, but we need to have backup on our tail," Johnson agreed.

"Let's get organized, and I'll gather up the boys."

"Okay, I'll meet you out front, Cap." Fowler jumped to his feet.

DONNA'S FEAR THAT HAD ONLY JUST SUBSIDED began to surge within her again. She watched Keller as he shoved the gun in his waistband and ripped the cookie package open. He had one cookie in his mouth and began to reach for another. With a burst of adrenaline, she tensed up and made her move. In one deft action, she snatched the razor-sharp knife, thrusting it with all of her might directly at Keller's neck. She felt the knife touch as she followed through. Keller extended his arm in an attempt to push her away. Unfortunately, the knife only grazed the side of his neck, slicing the top few layers of skin wide open. Blood ran from the entire length of the cut. She drew back, thrusting the knife in his direction on the return swing.

Keller felt the wind as the blade came within inches of his face. "Oh, you want to play again," he declared. He stepped toward her and, with a backhand, sent her to the floor along with a black eye. The knife flew from her hands on impact.

She was no match for the seasoned predator.

CHAPTER

SEVENTEEN

Rick planned to make one final stop Sheriff's residence. Deep in his heart, he hoped that he would knock on the door and old Bob would answer it and start lecturing him about being out in the elements when he should be home with Donna. Rose would invite him in for coffee, and he would tell them what he saw through the station window. Bob would suggest it was only his imagination. Darren and Avery had decided to 'get it on' on top of one of the desks, and now they were fast asleep. The three of them would sip their coffee and laugh and laugh.

Unfortunately, Rick sat on the snowmobile in front of the small yellow bungalow. The battered corpse of Avery lay on the desk. Visions of the carnage flashed through his mind. He took a deep breath and shook his head in an attempt to rid himself of the all-too-fresh memory and its atrociousness. The power was still out, but he could see that a fire was burning brightly in the fireplace, and several candles were lit here and there. He couldn't see anyone moving about inside, which led him to assume that whoever was home was either napping or eating a bite in the kitchen. Rick was scared to death to knock on the door, petrified that Bob was, indeed, one of the people dead in the bloodbath at the sheriff's office. This violent loss would haunt the townsfolk for years to come. He didn't know if he could face Rose at all.

Finally, he bucked himself up and got off the snow vehicle. He left it running and treaded his way through the drifted snow that obliterated the sidewalk leading to the front door. He couldn't make out any footprints Bob would have left behind that morning.

He stood on the porch and stared at the door, dreading the news he was going to have to share. Mustering all the courage he had in his body, Rick reached out and knocked. Rose's pleasant voice announced that she was coming.

The very sound of her sweet voice was enough for Rick to change his mind. He wasn't equipped to tell someone that their loved one was savagely murdered. The images of what he saw were too much for him to bear, let alone share. Besides, he wasn't even sure of himself anymore. What if Bob wasn't in there, and he'd gone with his truck plow to get help at the next town. What if all the cold and confusion messed with his mind. No,

Rick wouldn't say a word. As a matter of fact, he would be his usual self, if he could, anyway.

The door locks slid out of their places, and Rose Brown opened the door with a beaming smile. "Rick! What in the world are you doing out in this mess? Come in here right away! I have some coffee on the gas stove in my old percolator. Let's warm you up!"

She grabbed him by the arm and pulled him inside. He stood and stomped the snow from his boots and removed his coat. The warmth of the room was a relief. "Now, don't you give a fret about taking off them boots. Just come into the kitchen and sit down. To what do I owe the pleasure of your visit on this horrid day? You seem a bit off, Rick. What's going on?"

Rick smiled at her, but it didn't even come close to touching his heart. "Oh, not much. I see that Bob's not here. Is he up at the station dealing with the mess around here?" He had to change the subject, and he had to do it quickly, or he would break out in tears. He looked away from Rose while he sat, fixated on the fireplace watching the embers pop and crackle.

Rose put a piping hot cup of java in front of him, along with an old green sugar container and a teaspoon. "Yeah, well, you know they were putting up that stranger for the night. Bob said he would buy him a train ticket from the Pass to Rocky Mount, and he was going to pick him up and drive him to catch the train. Actually, I'm surprised I haven't heard from him. I mean, he hasn't even stopped by to let me know all is well. I can only assume he's busy plowing people out with that big ugly beast of his."

Rick's heart sank as he looked back in her direction. He sipped at the coffee, but it just made his stomach sicker. "I'm sure that's exactly what he's doing. I was stopping by to see if he'd plow my parking lot after the snow stopped. I'm guessing once the main road is clear, people are going to be heading our way for their little romantic winter getaways."

Rose sat across from him and stirred some sugar into her cup. "Yes. I always loved the thought of a winter escape with my Bob, but with his job and all."

"I know," he said. "I know."

The older woman studied him, concern in her eyes. "Are you all right? You look white as a ghost? Is Donna okay? Is she sick?"

He shook his head, no, and faked yet another smile. "She's fine. She took off for some staples from the store, but of course, nothing was open. I left before she got back to check on the other townsfolk, so I'm guessing she's home and warm by now."

"Well, son. You'd better drink that up and get home to her, or she'll have your hide if you make her worry too much."

He nodded and drained the cup, standing and giving a stretch for good measure. "Thanks for the coffee. Tell Bob to get a hold of me, will you?"

"Of course, and give Donna my love." The woman walked him to the door, then stood at the picture window and watched as he climbed on his snowmobile and took off. Rick stopped a block away. He couldn't be the bearer of the awful news. He just didn't have the heart to tell her. Rose would have died in front of him. He buried his head in his arms and cried. Oh, this heinous news was going to kill Rose when it all came out; it was already killing Rick. Thompson Trails was buried with a snowy massacre beneath it. They needed desperate help, and they needed it now.

———

As Rick rode away on the snowmobile, Rose kept her eyes on him until he was out of sight. Something was wrong. She knew it in her soul, but she couldn't quite figure out what was eating him. Nothing that came out of Rick's mouth matched the look on his face, but she'd never been one to force anyone to talk. But she was worried enough to try to get ahold of Bob again.

The house phone was dead, and Rose didn't keep a cell. The internet was still down, with no power, so that was useless. Rose stood at the picture window, wrapped in an afghan, and stared out for any sign of life that might come into view. Deep in her heart, she felt nothing but sorrow and gloom.

Captain Johnson rode shotgun in the massive plow truck driven by Detective Fowler. As they went, an old country song played low on the radio, muffled by the engine noise, but neither listened. Fowler was too busy clearing the roads for the troopers and their trucks following behind. All of the vehicles were taking the winding roads at very responsible speeds. Sure, this was an emergency, but the point was, it wouldn't do any good if someone were killed on the way to save the day.

"Are you sure that Sheriff Brown has this dirtbag?" Fowler asked for the tenth time.

Johnson groaned and nodded. "If I told you once, I told you a thousand times. Deputy Rush informed me that they had a vagrant matching his description perfectly, tattoos and all. I wouldn't be that concerned except an online nine-one-one came through, then disconnected. There's no reason for that coming from Thompson Trails, unless they have a mass murdering wacko in their custody. Something happened, Fowler, so stop making me repeat myself, will you?"

"I just don't want to get there and find out we all over-reacted." Who was Fowler trying to kid, anyway? The grisly slayer was on the prowl again.

Johnson flashed him a look. "I don't over-react, Jack." He worked a few high-profile cases over the years, and now here he was again. It was a matter of life and death.

The men continued in silence, pushing the snow and clearing the way for their backup. Johnson glanced at the clock on his cell phone; there was no signal. "At this rate, we should be there in an hour."

"Well, if you're right, I hope an hour is enough time before this monster continues to make history." Fowler had a concerned look on his face and a voice to match.

Johnson fought a frustrated tear. "I swear, threat or not. I'm going to put this rabid nut job out of his misery if I get the chance."

The men drove emotionally numb, just watching the windshield wipers thrashing about. Horrible scenarios plagued their minds. Yet, they were quiet, seemingly entranced from the engine drone and vibrations.

EIGHTEEN

T hings at the Virginia Trails Cabins had not improved in the slightest. Aside from Elliot Keller filling up on peanut butter by the spoonfuls and a package of old, outdated cookies, his mood had gotten worse. Donna's interpretation was that he was doing more than psyching himself up for whatever sick thoughts were running through his head.

He had tied her to the bed, and he had done a cruel job of it, to boot. Keller hadn't used rope or twine. Instead, he opted for some thick, braided metal wire that Rick used to secure the rental canoes to the docks. Keller found it with bolt cutters just strong enough to cut the lengths he needed. The thought of drawing blood from her soft porcelain skin excited him beyond belief. But more than that, the idea of her powerless husband watching him having fun while she bled turned him on even more.

"Where'd your man go?" he asked as he secured her painfully to the bed posters. "Maybe he decided you weren't worth coming back for. Maybe he thinks that you roped him into buying this dump, and now he's sick of the debt and heartache you're causing him with your pipe dreams."

Donna didn't bite. She simply stared at the ceiling, the expressions on her face consisting of the winces she produced when he tightened the wire.

"Nothing to say, huh, little bird?" Keller laughed and ran a length of wire around her midsection, pulling it tightly and securing it to the frame on the underside of the bed. She could swear it was cutting through her clothing and into her skin. She was already bleeding at the wrists and ankles. Nothing he did to her now would matter. Donna Welk had resigned herself to the fact that she would die, and she didn't care. She was emotionally numb.

"Well, he'd better hurry up," the man continued. "I'm running over to the shed to see what kind of fun toys I can find. I saw a cool saw in there that ought to make this the game of the century." Keller was sitting next to her right side on the bed, and he was smiling down at her. She met his eyes, appalled, and he caught it. It amused him even more. Bending over her, he winked and ran his tongue from her chin to her forehead. Her stomach lurched in disgust. The smell of his rotten breath reminded her of excrement, but she held on to her self-control. She wished she had thought to bite his tongue out of his mouth.

Sitting back up, he winked again. "See you soon, love." With that, he left, but he made a fairly big mistake. Keller was wearing an all-purpose tool on his waistband, a silver one with many little gadgets and knives. When he stood to leave, the device got caught on a tear in the quilt Donna was laying on, and it popped free without making a sound. He left unaware of his mistake. It was inches from her, and she had to find a way to get it.

She began to wiggle her hands around in the wire binds, but all that did was force the restraints deeper and deeper into her flesh. Blood ran down her arm, and though it was painful, it was of strange benefit. The blood greased up her arm and, pain or not, suddenly, her small right hand slid from the bind, ripping her skin wide open.

She grabbed the tool and used her mouth to open the cutters. Unfortunately, her hand was severely injured, and she couldn't squeeze the cutters hard enough to cut through the wire. The other wrist was extremely tight, and she couldn't reach her ankles. After struggling some more, she resorted to using her mouth to open up the large knife tucked away inside. A thrill of hope swept through her when she heard the blade snap into the open position. She tucked it under her body then fought her wrist back into the wire binding. It hurt worse to put it back than it had to remove, but she was past caring. The pain she felt was nothing compared to what he planned to do with her.

Donna hoped that Rick didn't return. She knew this guy's history, and he liked to make the men who loved the victim watch his horrific acts. Rick didn't deserve it, and she would rather die than have him see such things. Donna shook her head to rid it of the thoughts, then looked at her arm. The blood was dripping down to her elbow now, but it looked like it was slowing. She took a deep breath and went to a safe, secret place in her mind.

Ten minutes later, the door flew open, and Keller stepped inside. He carried a saw and a rusty old machete that Rick used to cut twigs for fires during the spring and summer months. She didn't want to think about what he intended to do with them, but she could imagine, and once again, she escaped to the confines of her mind.

Keller turned to the window with the sound of the snowmobile. Rick had returned. "Well, will you look at that? Mr. Rick Welk is here. It looks like he's ready to join the party. But he's going to have to find us first."

Donna groaned inside. She hoped against hope that this wouldn't happen. She had prayed that someone would come and save the day, but now she was sure how this story would end. Prayer hadn't done a thing for her; imagine that.

Donna's heart began to pound with both hope and fear. What were they going to do? Keller was ready for Rick. He had plenty of wire cut. A chair was positioned strategically across from where she lay bound along with a small pile of safety pins, for whatever reason. He also had a roll of duct tape, and to her, its use was pretty self-explanatory. She and her husband were going to die today.

Keller was peeking out through a small slit in the curtains. "He's going to the office," he said with a chuckle. "Maybe it was good that we left those candles on; he's sure to know you're here now. Just think, in minutes, the real fun and games will begin." He turned to her and grinned, his nasty front teeth repulsing her. "Are you as excited as I am, my sweet little lady?"

Keller continued to watch out the window and soon said, "Here he comes." He rushed over and slapped the silver duct tape to Donna's mouth. He put the tape on hard to show that he meant business and that she would be foolish to resist. Then he grabbed the bolt cutters he took from the shed as a weapon, ignoring the large flashlight lighting up the cabin. Keller positioned himself behind the cabin door, looked at Donna, and held a single finger to his lips to signify silence.

Donna fastened her swollen eyes on the door, and in a few seconds, the knob turned, and in stepped her husband. He instantly froze at the sight of her, panic filling his eyes. Donna tried to signal that Keller was behind the door, but Rick was so traumatized by the scene of his wife that he didn't notice. Rick rushed toward her, and Keller stepped out like lightning, hitting the man in the head. With a loud oof, Rick collapsed to the floor, completely unconscious.

Keller grinned again. "You two are way too easy. Well, on to phase two, wouldn't you say?"

CAPTAIN JOHNSON, DETECTIVE FOWLER, AND half of the State Patrol were just entering the Thompson Trails town limits. The panic in Johnson's stomach was tangible, but there was no time for weakness. He would have plenty of time to get sick later if his instincts were correct.

"Where to, Boss?" Fowler asked.

"The sheriff's office," he replied, stiffly. "It's right along this main drag, that much I know. This town's not very big. It'll be on the right, about two more blocks."

All the other trucks and police cars were moving in silence: no flashing lights, no sirens, nothing. The last thing Johnson wanted to do was incite panic in this tiny town or give the maniac warning of their arrival. All he wanted to do was make sure that his suspicions were either correct or wrong, whatever the case may be.

"There it is, the one with the buried snowmobiles."

Fowler pulled the plow over behind Donna's ski. The other vehicles pulled up single file behind Fowler, and Johnson got on the radio.

"No one gets out; the place looks dead. Fowler and I are going to approach first."

The two men crawled out of the big plow truck, drew guns, and approached the building. Johnson immediately tried the door, but Fowler went right to the window. He staggered back and could no longer hold down all the coffee he had ingested during the drive. He bent over and puked all over the pure white snow, melting it like salt in water. The horrific vision of the girl was enough to turn his stomach.

"Are you okay, man?" Johnson asked. "What's going on in there?"

Fowler wiped his mouth on the sleeve of his coat. "Dead. They're dead in there, and it's a bloody mess. Have the men get the battering ram. We have to get in there now."

The men did what they were told and beat the door in. On the third attempt, the door gave way, and all the men tumbled inside. The smell of blood was overwhelming. Three of the troopers had to go outside to up their coffee and donuts.

Fowler turned to Johnson. "That's the sheriff there, isn't it? Who's the woman?"

"I'm not sure. Let's clear the perimeter and make

sure there are no other victims." Johnson barked to all the officers.

"Fowler. Get on the police radio; we need a bus or two or three. Get the coroner here and as many cops as possible. Set up roadblocks. No one gets in or out. Notify the feds. We can only hope this sick scumbag hasn't gone too far, and that he's alone."

Unfortunately, they were all dead. The deputy was found in the far back closet. A broken framed photograph, probably dropped from the desk during the confrontation, was on the floor near where the girl lay splayed wide open. The picture seemed to confirm that she was the deputy's wife, and she had been horribly brutalized.

"Get a blanket out of that closet," Johnson directed the officers milling around, "Let's give this girl some dignity."

Fowler came running in. "We've got two buses coming from Donneley medical center and more backup on the way. They'll meet us here."

One of the officers returned with two blankets, which he used to cover the sheriff and the young woman. Johnson turned to Fowler and said, "We're going to find the sheriff's widow." He turned to the others. "All of you wait here unless I call for you. We have to find Mrs. Brown and figure out our next step."

With that, the two men tracked down the sheriff's address in the small Thompson Trails phonebook and took off in the plow. Both men dreaded the job they were about to do, but it had to be done. They were trained for it, but it was their least favorite part of the job. She might have some information that would help them find out where Elliot Keller might be. It was all they could hope for.

NINETEEN

I t was so hot! The heater had to be pumping out at a hundred degrees. Rick squirmed, trying to kick the blankets off his feet, but no matter how hard he tried, they remained covered and sweaty. The heat made him feel like he was sick with a very high fever. He groaned; why did he feel so weak? He couldn't even seem to muster the energy to climb out of bed and adjust the thermostat.

He was trying to say Donna's name, but his voice sounded muffled and low. Slowly, he became aware. There was a reason. Something was covering his mouth; something kept him from speaking.

Rick's eyes began to flutter, rapidly at first, then slower, until he found a way to open them all the way. He was confused, and his head was pounding. He wasn't in his bed; he was sitting in one of the chairs in his cabin.

Not only was he sitting in it, but he was also wired to it, or so it appeared. As he fought to clear his vision, he could feel blood trickling from the wounds that the taut wire created. His hands were bound behind his back, and wire was around his chest and waist. The wire on his legs was so tight it felt like it was touching the bone.

Now he looked up, and the first thing he saw brought a scream from the depths of his gut, but the scream stopped at the duct tape that covered his mouth. Donna was laying on the bed, wires binding her to the posters. She was beaten, or so it appeared. He could see cuts on her face that were crusted with blood, and like him, her wrists were bloody and sliced where the wires held her. She was staring at him with wide eyes, which she shifted now and then toward the bathroom.

His wife rapidly shook her head in an effort to tell him to stay quiet, but he was getting angrier and angrier with each passing second. It was all coming back to him in a rush now. The stranger he called Sheriff Brown about, the dead bodies at the station, his attempt to get ahold of the State Police over the computer which had failed miserably.

Movement from his left caught his eye, and he turned his head to see the perpetrator who was the cause of all of it. Rick began to struggle against the wire, but it just cut deeper into his skin with each movement, making him wince in pain.

"Uh, yeah, I wouldn't do too much of that if I were

you," the man said. "Keep going, and you'll do yourself in, and that would rob me of the pleasure, you see. So, sit still."

He paced between Donna on the bed and Rick in the chair, stopping after he had passed once between them. He had Rick's old rusty machete in one hand, and he was toying with the point of it with his forefinger. Rick kept his eyes focused on the guy's every move, his mind racing as he tried to figure out something, anything, he could do to save the lives of his wife and himself.

"I guess introductions are in order, Mr. Welk," the man said. "Donna and I have gotten pretty close. She knows me. At least, she knows me better than you do. My name is Elliot Keller. You might have heard of me; most people have."

Of course, Rick had heard of him. The guy was a murdering psychopath, but he was supposed to be in prison. How did this animal manage to get out of his cage? Rick's insides began to tremble with fear. Nothing about this situation pointed to a happy ending. It seemed to him that Keller was planning to do to Donna what he did to those three girls. They were the reason he was put away for life in the first place. Rick had to figure something out fast. He didn't want to watch his wife get tortured to death.

Keller continued. "I know a lot about you, Mr. Welk, and your pretty little wife." He sat down on the edge of the bed near Donna's head and shoulders but faced Rick and spoke. "Now, you should feel quite like the lucky one. You have a front-row seat to what's going to be the greatest show in history. The last one, well, we all know about that performance. This one will be close, but with just one woman, well, you might think the entertainment factor is a bit limited. No, don't kid yourself. Donna is quite a woman, aged to perfection, wouldn't you say? She's not a little teen like the last ones. They had no fight in them, and I tossed those girls around like little ragdolls. No, Donna gets me excited; I can't wait to see what she is hiding under these clothes."

Keller stood up and put the machete on the nightstand next to the bed. Out of his back pocket, he took out a hefty pair of silver scissors that Donna used for cutting material when she made the curtains for the cabins. He sat back down and took her shirt at the neck and began to cut it. Soon, it lay open, baring her milky white skin and bra. Next, Keller cut up each long sleeve, and at last, the top fell away and lay beneath her, forgotten. Rick began to thrash in earnest, ignoring the sharp pain that the wire was causing as it tore at his flesh.

Keller stood up and began to do something of a jig. Nothing fancy, just a couple of sloppy steps here and there. He had long black hair, and he had pulled the bangs and most of the top back into a ponytail. The rest of it dangled in long, greasy strands around his face. He smiled, did a twirl, and sat down at the foot of the bed. He began to take off her pink camouflage hiking boots, which caused her to cry out through the tape. The jerking motion he made as he removed the boots deepened the cuts of the wire on her ankles, and tears were streaming out of her closed eyes.

"We are going to have a bit of fun, the three of us," he said happily as he tossed one boot to the side, pulled off her thick wool sock, and started on the next boot. "I mean, I have to be honest, I'll be having the most fun, but I'm sure you'll be entertained enough by what you see that you'll be able to admit that you enjoyed it a bit."

The other boot came off, and Keller tossed it in the same direction as the first, then removed the other sock. He stood up and took a place next to Rick, grabbing him by his hair and jerking his head up, so he was forced to look at Donna.

"Open up, Mr. Welk, and get a good eyeful," Keller laughed. "I know, I know, it isn't much now, but just wait until we get those jeans off."

Rick clamped his eyes shut, frustration and fury filling him up. "I said, open them!" Keller punched him hard in the side of his head. Rick did as he was told and opened his eyes. "You know, I guess now is as good a time as any to take care of this whole eye thing."

The man walked away, and when he returned, he stood in front of Rick and held his hand open before him. Lying in the man's palm were two large safety pins. Rick looked at them, then looked up at Keller, confused.

"Oh, I see, you don't get it." Keller straddled Rick in

the chair and sat on his lap, facing him. The pain from the wire caused Rick to squirm in the seat. Keller watched him, amused. He looked deep into Rick's gaze to see the pain; Keller was enjoying every second of his agony. With a gleam in Keller's eyes, he spoke. "These are to help you, so you won't be tempted to close your eyes during the good parts. Now, it's going to hurt, believe me, but the more you struggle, the worse it'll be. And if you fight me, I swear, I'll do things to your wife that nightmares are made of. Well, I'm gonna do those things anyway, but I can make them completely horrible instead of just downright bad. So, sit still."

Keller placed one of the pins on the dresser directly behind Rick, then opened the other one. He wrapped his left arm tightly around the man's head to hold it in place, aimed the sharp tip of the pin at the man's eye, then paused. "This works best if you have your eyes part-way open, but you can close them if you want. I'll get the job done no matter what."

Rick knew what he was going to do, and his body wanted to fight, but his heart and mind were saturated with Donna. He bit the insides of his cheeks to prepare for the pain, which came fast. Keller stabbed the pin through Rick's left eyelid, gently yanked it open, then pierced the sharp tip through the man's eyebrow. Once it was all the way through the skin, he closed the pin and stood up to observe his handy work.

"Beautiful!" he gushed. "I must say, I've done this

many times in my life, but that is one of the cleanest and most attractive pinnings I've ever accomplished!"

It hurt! Blood was running down into Rick's eye, and the burning that the pin was causing was nothing short of torture. He couldn't blink or even come close to closing the eye; he just stared at the man and let his anger and fear keep him still.

"Time for the next!"

Keller grabbed the second pin and straddled him once more. The second eye went much faster, though it hurt a lot worse for some reason. Once again, he didn't struggle or fight. Rick just groaned in pain and controlled himself as best as he could. He didn't want to do anything that would make things harder on Donna.

When Keller stood, he fetched the scissors and danced around a bit more, humming what sounded like an old song of sorts. Scissors in hand, he pulled what appeared to be a dark blue scrub shirt over his head. That's when Rick noticed the man was wearing scrub pants as well. He was wearing clothes from the jail, and the realization made Rick recall Avery. The grisly horror was overloading his sanity.

Once the shirt was off, Keller kicked off his boots, walked to Rick, and bent down, putting his nose right against the man's. "Anyway, it's time to get back to Donna. I always love a good game of strip murder. It looks like I'm ahead of the game so far, wouldn't you say?"

Keller stood, spun around to Donna, whose eyes were filled with horror and anger, and held up the scissors, snapping them open and closed. "I think we'll go for the bra next. What do you say, pretty lady?"

CAPTAIN JOHNSON AND DETECTIVE FOWLER stood on the step of Sheriff Brown's quaint, modest home. They had just knocked and were waiting, soberly, for Mrs. Rose Brown to answer the door. They could both see her coming through the large picture window. She was a tiny, white-haired lady, and her bubbly, friendly personality was noticeable by how she carried herself. Fowler looked at Johnson, his eyes full of sadness; Johnson shook his head in return.

The main door opened, and Rose looked at the two men through the wrought iron framed screen door. The smile on her face disappeared instantly. Captain Johnson knew that the news of her husband's death had been told simply through eye contact.

"Mrs. Brown, my name is Captain Russell Johnson with the State Patrol. This is Detective Jack Fowler." He motioned to his companion. "May we come in, please?"

The woman didn't answer. She just opened the screen and held it for them as they crossed the threshold. They both began to stomp the snow off their shoes. Rose stopped them by touching them both on the arm.

"Never mind the snow. You can have a seat if you like." She walked into the living room. "I believe I know why you're here."

The men followed her and took seats in matching overstuffed chairs that went with the couch and loveseat in the room. Rose sat on the loveseat, and Johnson noted that a box of tissues was located right by where she was sitting.

"Mrs. Brown, this is never easy."

The older woman wrapped her arms around herself as if she was cold. "Men like you don't knock on the doors of people to announce things like block parties or potluck dinners at the church." She plucked a tissue but held it in her hand. "When and how did it happen?" Tears were already running down her face.

Fowler and Johnson glanced at each other, then Johnson replied, "Very early this morning, probably around dawn."

Rose nodded. "I assume it has something to do with that vagrant he was helping."

"Yes, ma'am."

More tears fell from her eyes, and she wiped them away, then straightened her shoulders and lifted her chin. "I always feared his career would end this way, but I took a bit of solace in the fact that this is such a small, safe town, you know?"

Neither of them answered; it was best just to let her talk at a time like this.

"So, who is this guy? This stranger that needed so much help?" Her voice was getting an edge to it, understandably. Her husband had gone out of his way to assist someone in need, and this was the result. Too trusting. Too kind.

This time, Fowler entered the conversation. "He is an escapee from Virginia Max. Elliot Keller. I know you haven't had power, so your husband had no way of knowing who he was." Rose put her hand to her mouth, signifying she knew Keller's history.

Johnson interrupted. "I called in the night and spoke to Deputy Rush to tell him about the escape, ma'am. We were calling every location directly. The deputy made us aware at that time that he believed he already had the suspect in custody. Unfortunately, we believe that the man overheard enough of the conversation to figure out that we were on to his location. I'm sorry to say that Darren is dead too."

"Does his wife, Avery, know?"

Fowler looked at his feet, so Johnson continued. "Ma'am, both the deputy and his wife are deceased. All three were found at the station house."

The two cops watched her eyes widen then glass over from shock. Rose placed her hands to her chest, crying in earnest. The men gave her the time she needed. She was a strong woman, though, and in a few minutes, she blew her nose and looked at them with red-rimmed eyes. "My lord, you boys, get out there and find this animal and put him down!" Her eyes were also filled with expectation, as if she knew there was more.

"Well?" she finally said. "I assume since you're still sitting here, there's a reason. Tell me?"

Johnson clasped his hands together and sat forward. "Ma'am, we have several reasons to believe that the man is still in or around Thompson Trails, and we think he has a hostage. We were just wondering if you could help us. Have you seen or heard anything that's out of the ordinary? Anything at all. We sure want to stop this maniac, but we need something solid to go by."

Rose thought for a minute. "I haven't left the house at all during the storm. Since Bob left for work this morning, the only person I've spoken to was Rick Welk. He stopped by, and I gave him a cup of coffee."

"Who is Rick Welk?" Fowler asked.

A couple of tears fell again, and Rose wiped at them with frustration. "Rick and his wife Donna own the Virginia Trails Cabins, just on the edge of town. They usually don't go visiting, but Rick said he just wanted to check on me to make sure I was okay." She went quiet for a moment, then continued. "You know, when he showed up unexpectedly, he was so sober, you know, serious. I asked him what was wrong, but he wouldn't say. He stayed for a moment, then left. You know, Bob told me that the stranger who was at the jail had been hanging around the cabins, and it was Rick who called to pick him up."

Now the two men exchanged long, knowing glances. "Where is the resort again, ma'am?" Fowler asked.

"Straight up the main road, that way. It's on the left; you can't miss it. About ten small cabins, with the lake right behind them. Cute little... oh, no! Do you think he's there?" She slowly lowered her arm from pointing in the direction.

Fowler and Johnson stood up. "Ma'am, once again, we're sorry for your loss, and we wish we could stay longer, but we have to find this man."

"Of course," she replied, following them to the door.

As they stepped outside, Fowler said quietly. "Please, stay inside and keep things locked up. If your phones come on, call around and tell everyone to do the same."

"You boys put him down this time!" She watched the men as they made their way to the large plow truck and climbed inside.

Johnson got on the radio and called for the men at the sheriff's office. "We're going to need all available officers for back-up at the Virginia Trails Cabins on the north end of town, and we need them right away. We have reason to believe Keller is there with two hostages. One Donna and Rick Welk."

Fowler pulled the truck out and headed up the road. "You think he's there, huh?"

Johnson stared straight ahead, his hand on his gun. "I know he is."

TWENTY

hen Johnson and Fowler were sitting in Rose Brown's living room, Keller was finishing up removing Donna's clothing. The woman now lay, bound and bleeding, bare naked as the day she was born. Her husband watched, helpless and heartbroken, as blood and tears ran around his eyes and down his face. In his hands, Keller had a saw, the machete, and a couple of steak knives from the kitchen. He told them with amusement that he needed two because blades like that broke so easily.

It became increasingly evident to Donna that he had forgotten the multi-purpose tool, and she wasn't about to remind him of it.

Keller walked around the bed, passing back and forth. "Now, let's play a game. I'm going to ask a series of questions, and you, Rick, will answer them. There is no need to remove the tape; they will all be yes or no answers. Donna gets a poke or a cut with one of my fun little tools if you get them wrong. If you get them right, well, she gets a big old poke with my main tool, in the orifice of my choosing. Sound like fun?"

Rick shook his head madly and began to try and scream against the tape. Keller took one of the steak knives and stabbed it clean through the sole of Donna's right foot. She screamed and cried, her body arching against the wire at her midsection, digging into the flesh and making her bleed more. When he pulled the knife out, the tip broke off and stuck slightly out of her foot.

"This is what I mean by a poke, just so we are clear. Now choose wisely." He said with composure and a knit brow.

Rick tried to calm himself, and his eyes sought out Donna's, but hers were clamped shut against the pain, tears continued to run down her face. If he could get his hands on this guy, he would butcher the demented maniac with the machete.

"So, let's play," Keller began. "First question: the male victim who survived the cabin attack that sent me to prison; was his name, Teddy?"

Rick's mind immediately went to the more than five-year-old crime, and he tried to pull up the details, but they hadn't lived in Virginia then. Sure, it made national news all around the United States, but still. Regardless, the name 'Teddy' didn't ring any kind of bell at all.

"Tick-tock, tick-tock."

Rick had to answer. He had to take a chance, even though it was a losing situation either way. He began to nod yes furiously.

"Wrong answer!"

Keller ran to the side of the bed and plunged the broken knife into Donna's left arm, then pulled it out forcefully. Another round of tears and taped-up screams. Along with a stream of blood that saturated the bed beneath her arm.

Keller ignored their screams and began to walk around the bed again. "Question number two: was I born in Georgia?"

Rick's eyes searched his face for any kind of sign that would give away the answer, but the guy was so busy smiling and dancing around that there was no way to read him. Rick watched as Keller put down the broken knife and picked up the machete, then ran his finger gently along the blade.

"Time's running out, Rick."

Rick nodded 'yes' another time.

"Wrong again! I'm a Virginia boy all the way!"

Keller took the machete and pressed the blade hard against the bare skin of Donna's right thigh. He dragged it, going deeper as he went, just hard enough to make her bleed. Keller watched the seeping blood as it oozed down the side of her leg. Donna was getting pale, and this time she didn't scream. She whimpered, her body and mind growing weak. Rick, however, continued to holler against the tape.

Keller stopped cutting at her knee. "This thing's a lot sharper than it looks, isn't it? I think I'm gonna have to keep this as a souvenir."

He turned to Rick for the third time. "Question number three, and believe me, I can't wait for you to get one of these right. I am so hard that I might explode if I don't put it somewhere soon. Question three: am I an only child?"

Rick stared at him. He was sure the guy had siblings of some kind. He didn't want Donna to lose any more blood, but worse than that, Rick didn't want this freak to rape her, and a correct answer would result in just that. He knew what answer he was going to pick. He would nod yes, that Keller was an only child.

"Hurry up, Ricky-boy," Keller whispered in his face. "Don't want time to run out, do you?"

Rick held his breath, looked the nutcase in the eye, and gave a firm nod 'yes.'

"Bing-bing-bing! You are correct! Finally! Time for the real stuff!"

Rick continued to scream through the tape repeatedly.

At the entrance to the Virginia Trails Cabins sat Fowler and Johnson in the pickup plow, with the ignition off. Four other State Patrol trucks sat lined up alongside them, all with the lights out and engines off as well. They were watching the only cabin with lights creeping through the pulled blinds: the cottage that Rick and Donna Welk called home.

Captain Johnson was communicating with the men over the police band radio. The plan was to have a group, led by him, sneak around the back of the cabin and surround it, while the others blocked the driveway entrance and the property's perimeter. They were all armed, vested, locked, and loaded, but they wouldn't make a move to enter until they were sure someone was inside. So far, all they could see was the sliver of light through the drawn curtains. All it would take was a single peep, and they would barnstorm the place.

"Okay, gentle with the car doors. We don't want him to know we're here." Johnson looked at Fowler, who would mind the men taking care of the perimeter. "The rest of you, don't make a move without Fowler's say, got it? And boys, shoot to kill." Johnson released the button, and the radio squawked.

Ten-four came back in unison.

Checking his gun for the hundredth time, Johnson gave one more look at the detective next to him, then got out of the vehicle and closed the door gently enough just to latch it. It barely made a sound. All the troopers joining him followed suit, and together, they made their way around the back of the main office and to the rear of the Welks' cabin.

Soon, the group reached their mission point and split up surrounding the cottage. They sidled up against each side of the cabin. The men stopped just out of sight along the sides of the small building. But Johnson crept, kneeling, under the window and to the door.

He didn't need to wait for long. The first thing Johnson heard was the muffled screams of pain and horror in two different voices. He listened to the laughter of a crazed Elliot Keller, who sounded like he was having the time of his life. Johnson shot a look up to the other men. From what he could hear, they were still alive. He looked to the left side of the cabin and made eye contact with the lead man there, signaling with the tilt of his head and a gesture. Then, Johnson did the same to the right. Once he was sure all the men were ready, with a jerk of his head and a pointing motion of his hand, Johnson stood, gave the door a solitary violent kick, and rushed inside, his entire team at his heels.

What they saw inside that cabin would haunt their dreams for the rest of their lives.

TWENTY-ONE

At the same time, the state troopers were discussing strategy on the police band radio, Rick correctly answered the question regarding Elliot Keller's only child status. As it turned out, answering the question accurately was the worst thing Rick had ever done, and now his wife Donna was being given the grand prize.

Keller had removed all of his clothing, then positioned himself on his knees between Donna's spread legs. He was laughing and telling a story of a time he was blamed for misbehavior, and he was graphically describing the punishment he received. Before her shock and surprise gave way to a scream. Keller was on top of her, pressing against her chest with his entire body weight. "And now for the coup de grâce," he hollered with great, flamboyant gestures. With one powerful thrust, he was inside her, and Donna was helpless to do anything but allow the rape to go on. As he did so, Keller held a lit cigarette to various parts of Donna's body, ignoring her muffled screams, as well as those of her horrified husband.

But instead of continually pumping away, Keller held his position, burned her a couple more times, then tossed the cigarette on the nightstand, where it lay burning the surface of the wood. Keller picked up the machete lying next to Donna's thigh on the bed, then he drew back with one arm, brought it forward, and lightly sliced an extended diagonal cut from her right shoulder to the opposite hip bone. Now the screams came, loud and clear as an alarm going off. The incision began to bleed profusely, but Keller paid the blood no mind. Thankfully for Donna, the cut wasn't too deep. His head was thrown back, his mouth wide open in ecstasy as his body responded to the violence that turned him on so much.

Rick sobbed helplessly, his face soaked in sweat and tears. Never had he felt so powerless as a man in his life. Rick wanted to die. Keller was acting out a brutally sadistic scene he had imagined many times before. What kind of psychopath wanted to do this?

Donna's eyes went to her right wrist, the one she had slid out of the wire before. She glanced at Keller and noticed he was looking up. Rick was forgotten, and so was she at the moment, but she had no idea how long that would last. Slowly, Donna pulled her arm down through the loop. It hurt like hell, and she realized that the flesh had swollen. She was past the point of caring. Donna continued to pull with a bit more pressure each second until it seemed to be blinding her. She tugged, and the blood began to flow once again. The sound of her skin ripping made her bite down hard, gritting her teeth. Her right hand suddenly slid free. Donna held it up anyway, just in case movement would make him look at her. Then, millimeter by millimeter, she put her hand down and slid it under her.

There it was: the tool with the knife out. Donna watched Keller as she wrapped her hand around its handle. Donna glanced at her husband and mouthed the words, 'I love you.'

As fast as lightning, she pulled the knife out and buried it deep in his flesh, right about his pubic hairline. Holding on with an iron grip, Donna gave the knife a yank upward cutting until the blade hit his ribs, then she jerked it down again. Blood poured from him, pouring all over her, but Donna was smiling and looking at his eyes.

Elliot Keller looked back, shock and surprise written all over his face. The machete, which he had been holding in mid-air, fell onto the bed behind him. His surprise quickly turned to rage. But Donna didn't hesitate to do more damage. She wanted him to die. She pulled the knife out and drove it into his thigh, yanked it back out, and watched as an incredible stream of blood shot across the room from his now-severed femoral artery.

Keller looked down, and his hands fell limply to his sides. The man was beginning to weave back and forth, and even though he was still staring at Donna, his focus was waning. He was going to die right on top of her.

The door flew open with a loud crash, as though a bomb had gone off. Policemen poured into the cabin, guns drawn, all focused on the madman who still had his member buried inside Donna Welk's battered body.

Gunfire rang out and filled the room. A sharp shooter had no problem finishing Keller off, spraying blood and brains all over the walls.

"You sick freak!" Russell Johnson's voice was deadly, determined, and filled with disgusted rage. "I swear, get him off of her, now!"

Rick sat frozen to the chair, his eyes wide as saucers and the safety pins forgotten, even as they assisted him in his stare. He watched Keller closely to see what the man was going to do.

Johnson spoke through grit teeth. "No second chance this time, scumbag."

"Get him off me!" Donna screamed. "Get him off!"

The men moved faster than her eyes could register, and in seconds, they had one dead Elliot Keller lying on the floor.

TWENTY-TWO

The next day

"**M**r. Welk, I can't imagine how you feel, and we just want you to know how sorry we are for what you and your wife have gone through."

Rick lay in a hospital bed in Donneley's Pass, pillows propping him up to make him as comfortable as he could be. All the dope they pumped in him was making him physically comfortable, but it wasn't easing his tormented mind and heart when he thought of his wife.

"I'm sure you're sorry," he responded in a sad but polite voice. "I appreciate it, but save your breath, remorse, and compassion for my poor wife."

Captain Johnson and Detective Fowler were sitting in vinyl hospital chairs in Rick's private room. Except for some scrapes, bruises, a concussion, and some small, scabby holes on his eyelids and forehead, the man was in pretty good shape, physically, anyway.

Rick looked at him, then at Fowler, with a look of defeat in his eyes. "You know, I always knew there were people like that in the world, like Keller. But they're never real to you. They aren't typically the type of people you encounter. They're like phantoms, the kind of ghosts that are in nightmares."

The two cops listened patiently and quietly, and Rick continued. "The things he did to my Donna, my sweet Donna, and right before my very eyes." Tears began to fall, and Rick found himself thankful for the greasy balm they had put on his eyelid wounds. It didn't stop the pain completely, but it helped the sting of the tears just a bit.

"How is she?" he asked. "At least, since the last time you were up there."

"She's heavily sedated," Fowler answered quietly. "We can't pursue a report yet, not that it matters; the bastard is dead."

"Maybe there will be some changes made at good old Virginia Max. How a convicted murderer ever gets enough privileges to get anywhere near a door in a maximum-security prison is beyond me."

The three men remained silent until Dr. Frazer entered the room. "Hello, Mr. Welk. How are you feeling?"

"Aside from my mangled pride and broken heart, I'll be okay," he replied. "I want to know about my wife."

The physician looked at the two cops. "Would you mind stepping out while I speak with my patient?"

Rick straightened up, a determined look on his face. "No! I want them to stay. I want them to hear what this man did to my wife."

The doctor nodded with resignation. "Okay. She has severe cuts and stabs, a couple of which required surgery. Donna will have full use of her hand and foot. She has a concussion, likely from a blow he gave her to the head, so the sedative she is on is very mild. We don't want her getting too sleepy. Also, um, she suffered some internal damage from the sexual assault, but pain medication is helping with that. She needs lots of rest, but she's going to make it. She's one tough cookie, Mr. Welk, but I would highly recommend some therapy after this. She has been through hell and back."

"When can I see her? And how soon do you think it will be before she can help these guys file a report?"

Dr. Frazer shrugged. "I think we need to give it a few days. I have to look out for her well-being. Forcing her to recall the trauma too soon could be detrimental."

"I understand," Rick gestured in agreement.

The doctor nodded. "Good. I promise I'll let you know as soon as you can visit her, and the police will be notified when she is well enough to give a report. I'll check back in on you later. Try to rest."

The man left the room, and Johnson looked up at Rick. "It's going to be okay. Maybe not right away, but it will be okay. It will pass."

"I know," Rick said wearily. "Everything passes, doesn't it?"

Fowler cleared his throat. "I assume you won't be going back to the resort when you leave here?"

Rick shook his head. "Actually, Rose Brown invited us to stay with her for the time being, at least until we hire a company to clean up the resort and get it on the market. I'll never take her back there. I'll pick up sentimental and important things. Otherwise, I think staying with Rose is going to be the best thing for all three of us."

"I would have to agree," Johnson said with a nod.

With that, the two troopers stood and gingerly shook Rick's hand, trying not to irritate his scabbing and swollen wrist wounds.

"We're both going to be staying at a hotel here at the Pass," Johnson said. "Don't be afraid to call us for any reason." Both men set their cards on the nightstand next to Rick's bed. "Our cell numbers are on there. Even if you just need to talk, okay?"

Rick nodded. "Thanks for saving our lives, guys. I'm just sorry it wasn't me that killed him."

Fowler nodded. "I think everyone who was in that room feels the same way."

The men gave Rick a final sympathetic nod and left.

Rick took one of his extra pillows and put it over his sore, swollen face. As soon as he did, he began to sob like a little boy, flashes of what Keller did to his wife torturing his mind. But worse yet, he would be forever tortured for being unable to help her. Rick let it happen, and for that, he could never forgive himself.

TWENTY-THREE

Two months later

For the first time in a long time, Donna had a smile on her face, and this made Rose happy. Even though she was still pretty bandaged up and a bit swollen, her stitches had been removed, and she was beginning to look more like herself. "Rose, I think I have everything I want from the resort. I don't think Rick needs to go back. I feel like he's doing all the work, plus he's been so good about taking care of me. Sometimes I feel guilty about it."

Rose patted her on the shoulder. "Just try to understand the guilt he's been feeling, dear. It's almost incomprehensible."

Donna understood the grief. In fact, it was incredibly distressing to know that her husband carried around the undue burden of blame because he couldn't do anything to stop the violent onslaught. But they were in it together. Keller tortured Rick in more ways than one as well. Donna had been so upset by the trauma and aftermath that she was consistently ill since the incident. Many times a day she ran to the bathroom to vomit. But in the last couple of weeks, Donna was beginning to feel better. She continued to be victimized by terrible flashbacks, and she woke up with horrible nightmares more often than not. But she was getting some of her strength back.

Now, she sat with Rose, drinking coffee and finally going through the boxes that Rick had packed up and brought to her from the resort. As she had said, it appeared he had gotten every last item she wanted; the rest was left behind to be disposed of, along with the terrible ghosts that now haunted the place, thanks to Keller.

A stack of new boxes was piled along a wall in Rose's dining room. Together, the two women were busy going through the scant possessions the Welks had decided to keep. They were packing things up to move into their new home, a small rancher about five miles out of town. Rick took an assistant manager position at the grocery store. Donna decided to take on some accounting work from the comfort of home since she had her CPA anyway. Plus, she now had a slight fear of leaving the house for anything more than errands, and she didn't even like to run those by herself. Yes, working from home was the solution for her.

Rick was transporting boxes and other small items to their new home while the women worked. He would pile more stuff into the small rental truck with each return trip. Rose gave them a few items of furniture that she kept stored in an oversized garage out back, and all of these things pretty much gave the Welks a brand-new start. They all hoped it would be a new beginning filled with much better memories.

———

"DONNA, DON'T FORGET ABOUT THAT appointment you have this afternoon with Dr. Frazer," Rose said with a motherly tone, as she sipped her coffee. "I know you're feeling better, but in this situation, I think it's imperative that you follow through, dear. Who knows? Maybe he'll take you off of all those anxiety pills you hate so much."

Donna glanced at her watch. "Yes, I should jump into the shower, I suppose. Listen, Rose, don't you worry a thing about all of this stuff. When I get home, I'll get back to work, and soon the two of us will be out of your hair." She turned to Rose and took her in for an embrace.

"You're not a burden," Rose said. "You know as well as I do that I wouldn't have made it through all of this myself without you and Rick."

"I know, we love you, and we're here for you too." Donna gave the woman a peck on the cheek and disappeared into the bathroom for her shower.

Rose paused to wipe the tears from her eyes. Even though time passed, and time healed all wounds, she sure wasn't quite there yet. And something was off about Donna, but she couldn't seem to put a finger on it. She and Donna had spent the day packing and sorting, but Rose could tell something was off with the young lady. She saw a sadness in her eyes on several occasions, and Rose would ask if all was well. Donna would quickly smile, nod, and crack some senseless, though funny, joke. She was good at changing the subject every time.

<hr>

AN HOUR LATER, DONNA WAS LEAVING THE house with Rick, who had returned for the sole purpose of driving her to her appointment in Donneley's Pass. Contrary to what she had been told, Rose continued to tinker and organize boxes for the young couple, who she now thought of as her own children. The woman cried as she went about the task; the fact was, it was breaking her heart for them to leave, even if they were moving only a few miles away.

<hr>

Rick sat in the waiting area at Dr. Frazer's office, awaiting his wife with a copy of an old magazine. He was carelessly flipping the pages every few seconds. His mind was on Donna. After all of the torment and trauma, she had been a mess, and her state of mind, including physical sickness, had lasted nearly two whole months. She seemed cheerful recently, so he was taking this as a positive sign.

The door leading to the back opened up, and Donna stepped out. She looked a bit flushed, and when she saw Rick, a smile covered her face. He smiled back and stood up, quickly making his way over to her.

"Are we done?" he asked.

"Dr. Frazer wants me to make a follow-up appointment." She replied gently. "If you want to go warm the car, I'll be out in just a bit." Rick nodded and left, Donna watching him as he went.

Rick looked through the passenger window facing the building, waiting for Donna. Within minutes she emerged, and he quickly made his way around the car as Donna approached.

"Hello, love," she said softly.

"So, what did Dr. Frazer say?" Rick asked as he kissed Donna firmly on the lips.

"Well," Donna replied lightly, "he thinks I'm doing better, both mentally and physically. He even took me off the drugs, for now at least."

"Great! So, what's the follow-up for?" Rick closed

the passenger door, and he quickly made his way around the car. When he opened the door, Donna was sitting up on the seat with a folded piece of paper.

Donna didn't smile at him, and though he noticed this, it didn't register.

"I take it you have some pretty big news."

She nodded, then gestured with her left hand to the piece of paper. "I have something for you to read."

Rick closed the door and picked up the neatly folded sheet. "What's this?"

"You'll have to read it and find out."

The tone of her voice concerned him; something wasn't right. Slowly, he unfolded the paper and read, and as he did, his heart began to beat so hard he thought he might pass out.

"Is this true?"

She didn't answer. She just stared at his face, bewilderment and despair in her eyes, but not a single tear fell.

"How can this be?"

His wife didn't even shrug. Instead, she shook her head, and her eyes began to glass over. "All I can say is, after all the trying and failing, that monster managed to get the job done."

According to the paper, Donna was pregnant, and she and her husband hadn't had sex since late October. The child belonged to Elliot Keller. The child was the offspring of a maniac.

Panic began to well up in Rick's throat. The piece of paper fell from his hand and fluttered to the floor. He was dumbfounded. For several years the couple tried to have children. Was this a miracle or some unfathomable nightmare? He grabbed her hands and stared at his beautiful wife, perplexed. "It will be okay. We'll have an abortion; we'll take care of this."

"No," Donna said somberly.

Rick wanted to have kids just as much as Donna did. After a few moments of silence, Rick spoke. "I have to tell you, you are the strongest woman I know, and I couldn't be more blessed to have you for a wife."

"I feel the same way about you, my love."

Donna glanced at him continually out of the corner of her eye. Even though it felt like the world was crashing down around them, yet again, Donna wanted to keep the baby. They would find a way to make it work and love the child unconditionally. They'd ensure the child was adequately nurtured to end the abusive cycle that plagued Keller's family. The Welks would do everything they could to guarantee the child grew up to be a decent human being.

That's all it took, right? A little love?

ENTREATY

This book was made possible by reviews from readers like you. Reviews fuel my creativity. If you enjoyed this novel, I implore you to write a review and share your experience on the retailer's website. Please tell a friend or loved one, who may also like to give this heart pounding book a read! In return, I thank you from the bottom of my heart, and sincerely appreciate your time and effort.

Humbled, with gratitude,
R.W.K. Clark

ABOUT THE AUTHOR

I am a father of two beautiful children, Jon and Kim. They are my motivating forces. They are the lighthouse in this vast ocean. In my life, they are the air that I breathe, the oasis in this desert of uncertainty. They are my greatest joy in life and my number one priority. I have a long list of hobbies, and I attribute that to my lust for life! I like to surround myself with positive people who share the same interests. Family values, the arts, outdoors, nature, and travel are tops on my list. I embrace attending cultural and artistic events because I believe dramatic self-expression is the window to the soul. I wear my heart on my sleeve, and I still believe in chivalry, and I always treat people the way I want to be treated.

www.rwkclark.com

Printed in Great Britain
by Amazon